HORATIO CLARE

THE PRINCE'S PEN

OR CLIP'S TRUTH

NEW STORIES FROM THE

MABINOGION

SEREN

D0273886

NEATH PORT TALBOT LIBRARIES	
2300033480	
ASKEWS & HOLT	01-Nov-2011
AF	£8.99
Pon	

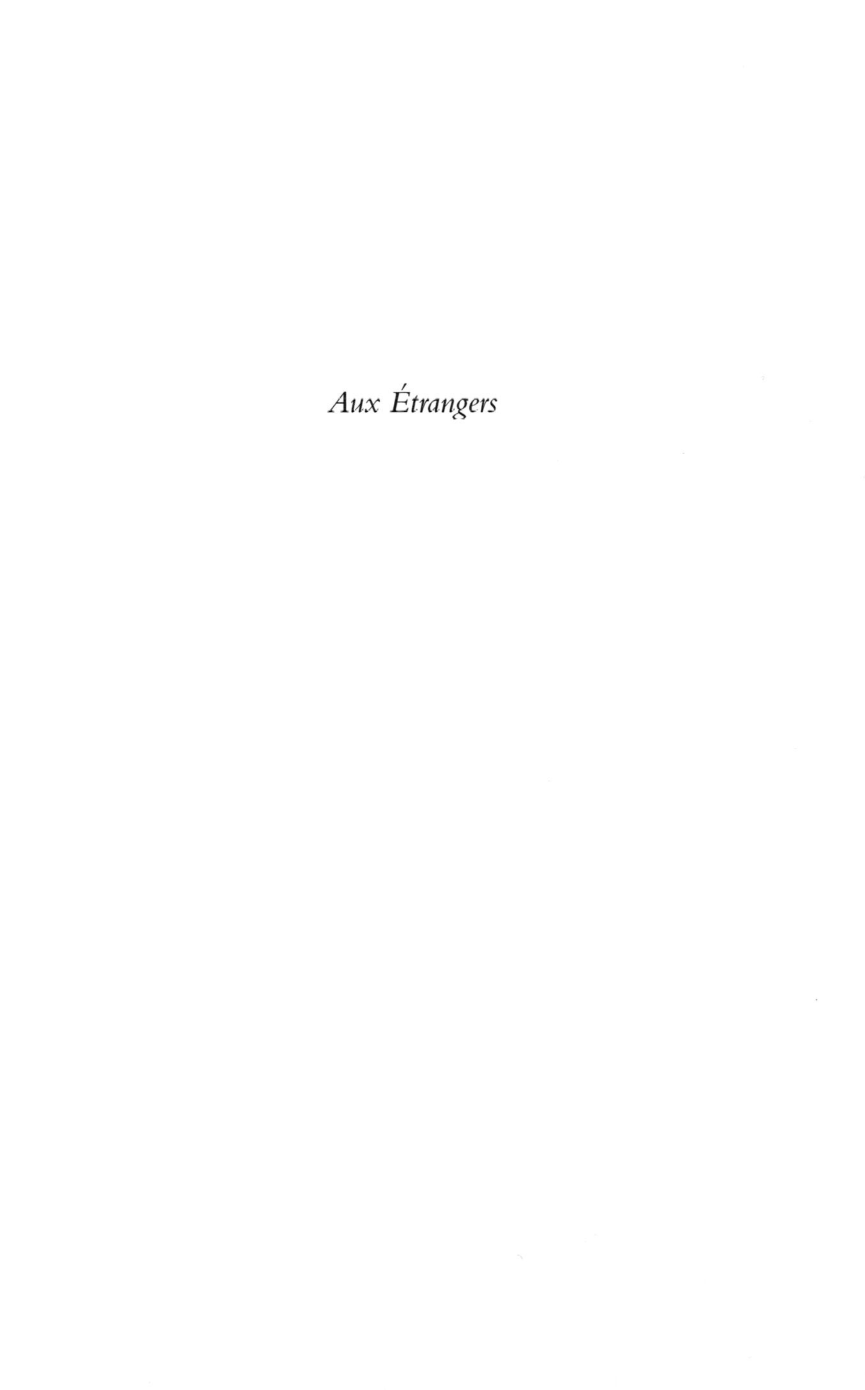

Aux Étrangers

Seren is the book imprint of
Poetry Wales Press Ltd
57 Nolton Street, Bridgend, Wales, CF31 3AE
www.seren-books.com

© Horatio Clare 2011

ISBN 978-1-85411-552-2

The right of Horatio Clare to be identified as the author of this work has been asserted in accordance with the Copyright, Designs and Patents Act, 1988.

A CIP record for this title is available from the British Library.

All rights reserved. No part of this publication may be reproduced, stored in a retrieval system, or transmitted at any time or by any means electronic, mechanical, photocopying, recording or otherwise without the prior permission of the copyright holder.

This book is a work of fiction. The characters and incidents portrayed are the work of the author's imagination. Any other resemblance to actual persons, living or dead, is entirely coincidental.

Cover design by Mathew Bevan

Inner design and typesetting by books@lloydrobson.com

Printed by Bell and Bain, Glasgow

The publisher acknowledges the financial support of the Welsh Books Council.

Contents

New Stories from the Mabinogion

Introduction

Some stories, it seems, just keep on going. Whatever you do to them, the words are still whispered abroad, a whistle in the reeds, a bird's song in your ear.

Every culture has its myths; many share ingredients with each other. Stir the pot, retell the tale and you draw out something new, a new flavour, a new meaning maybe. There's no one right version. Perhaps it's because myths were a way of describing our place in the world, of putting people and their search for meaning in a bigger picture that they linger in our imagination.

The eleven stories of the *Mabinogion* ('story of youth') are diverse native Welsh tales taken from two medieval manuscripts. But their roots go back hundreds of years, through written fragments and the unwritten, storytelling tradition. They were first collected under this title, and translated into English, in the nineteenth century.

The *Mabinogion* brings us Celtic mythology, Arthurian romance, and a history of the Island of Britain seen through the eyes of medieval Wales – but tells tales that stretch way beyond the boundaries of contemporary Wales, just as the 'Welsh' part of this island once did: Welsh was once spoken as far north as Edinburgh. In one tale, the gigantic Bendigeidfran wears the crown of London, and his severed head is buried there, facing France, to protect the land from invaders.

There is enchantment and shape-shifting, conflict, peacemaking, love, betrayal. A wife conjured out of flowers is punished for unfaithfulness by being turned into an owl, Arthur and his knights chase a magical wild boar and its piglets from Ireland across south Wales to Cornwall, a prince changes places with the king of the underworld for a year…

Many of these myths are familiar in Wales, and some have filtered through into the wider British tradition, but others are little known beyond the Welsh border. In this series of New Stories from the Mabinogion the old tales are at the heart of the new, to be enjoyed wherever they are read.

Each author has chosen a story to reinvent and retell for their own reasons and in their own way: creating fresh, contemporary tales that speak to us as much of the world we know now as of times long gone.

Penny Thomas, series editor

The Prince's Pen

Part One

So now you want to know how we won the war, and the peace – and what happened to the money? Not that you'd have cared for a word of mine if you'd been there at the beginning! Not that I said much to anyone but him. Oh, they had names for me. His Nun, his Freak; they hated me... and I never drank so when he stopped they hated me, and they hated me because they knew there was *something* and I would never let on.

I never let on that Ludo the Warlord, the Prince of the West, the Master of the Severn Sea, the Codfather himself, could neither read nor write. There, I've said it: Ludo had the literacy of a lamb. And thanks to me he needed no letters, for as he used to say, he had his Clip, the Prince's Pen! Everything he needed to remember and hold to him he kept stored in that red-curled head. Anything he must read or write fell to me. No one else was ever close to me, after he took me on.

They thought it was my looks, my curled and tortured face, poor Cut-lip Clip, which kept my bed so cold. But it never was just that. There were soft girls and hard girls who might have reached for me, and perhaps not just for my access to him; women who might have nailed their palms in the darkness and steered their tongues aside my scar-split face – but I could not have them. The spiters were right: I was his Nun, a bride of our battles. (The only one I loved, beside him, I could never have.) And now that he is gone, and his little empire in the care of the daughter of his brother, the great Levello, the Mountain King, and because I have time before I go...

Here is the story of Ludo and Levello. Here is the true history of how, by cunning and valour, they defeated the Invaders. Here is how Ludo – through his brother's counsel and Uzma's power – mastered the dread beast of Faith. And here also is a curious chapter in Ludo's last coup, the restoration of the people's land. From Clip the Prince's Pen, last survivor of the court of Ludo the Warlord, the Peace Father, to you, unknown reader of the future, Greetings!

Now, to begin: have your historians told you why the Invaders came? They said we harboured their enemies. (That was barely half true: they were small sprats, those Dissenters.) They said we were backward, out of the times, savage obstacles in the path of progress and peace, an offence to the United Nations and World Majority Government.(That was a little more true – what were their distant councils to us? What were their rabbles of waggling jaws, their assemblies of unimaginable bureaucrats? They were nothing.) But no, no. The prize was not a few chanting ascetics, nor the conversion of a bunch of farmers and fishers and smugglers to their one-party faith and their God, ICU. The prize was elemental. Our air, our west winds and our rain-making hills: water! We were near drowned in it half the time, though not so nearly as our poor neighbours, the English.

By the time the Invaders arrived our land was already a groaning ship and England a dense archipelago, a shattering of islands written thick with silver runes. Cities drawn up like anchored ships: sea towers, flood walls, residential rigs, quays and miles of bridges. They called it New Venice. It sounds romantic but in old Wales we knew we were lucky to have our feet on steep stone, green slopes and earth.

Shipping was the business you wanted then. Young men with hopes to catch headed for the docks like gulls. Ludo and Levello were born within sniff of the sea, as I was. They came from a farming family, four brothers up on the rise above Druidstone. Ninnian and Caswallawn stayed on the farm. Levello, at thirteen, went north to the new harbour at Aberystwyth. Ludo, two years older and ever a man for the most direct move, came south to Pembroke Dock. He found work on the flying-boat fleet, with the Longshore Union, and that is how we met.

I was born in Castle Terrace, Pembroke. We knew Ludo before he knew us, a red barrel of a boy, never silent, with a prodigious memory for a face and a cargo and jokes. My father was a doctor with the Port Inspectorate. Every foreign boat that landed, every duck with a load and crew had to be inspected. It was remorseless work, my father's share enough for five. (Almost all the doctors, engineers and brains went East, of course, to the money and the good living.) At fifteen I was two years his assistant. 'Jelly-fish' they called me in those days, and 'Porto', after the Portuguese Man O'War.

'Looks like a jelly that sucked a propeller!'

My father's operation, his one and only attempt at cosmetic surgery, did not help much. I was marked an easy target, and would have stayed one if only the Piranhas, the little quayside knife boys, had not tried to rob me, under that old blue moon.

My father had taken delivery of a box of vaccines from India and I was hill-hauling them back to our store when the Piranhas struck. All around me in a moment.

'Give it up!'

'Get away. It's no good to you.'

'Give it up or you're gutted!'

Out came the knives.

'It's vaccine!' I cried, 'You can't use it! Let me by, I'll give you money.'

'We'll have the money as well.'

From utter darkness in the wing of shadow behind the Flying Pilot there came a rush of splatter like a horse pissing, and a voice.

'I know you, Skinny Jakes,' it said, 'You *know* I know you.'

The Piranhas stopped. One squealed: 'Who's that? Get out of there!'

The pissing continued prodigious. A black snake wound down the road.

'Who's this!' There was a laugh and the voice had form now, a shape more man than boy. 'This is the King of Old Pembroke Town and he's telling you to scat!'

The pissing stopped, there was a shuffle-pause and a slow *zii-p*.

'Now,' said Ludo, stepping out of the shadow with his fists up like monkeyheads, 'who's got the liver to wash my hands? Does it have to be you, Skinny Jakes?'

The Piranhas shoaled at him and there was a crack as he flattened one, a blurred thud and another was limp, his weedy body Ludo's shield, preventing the rest from using their knives.

'You'll drop it or your Jakes is cut and I'll take his blade to the rest of you,' said Ludo, terribly calmly. He did not sound breathless or even the merest bit excited, that was the frightening thing.

'Aww, Ludo! Let him go!'

'Fair's fair boys, and goodnight to you!' boomed Ludo, jetting the woozy body at them. In a scrabble there were only the two of us, and the body he'd hit lying still. I was standing there, holding the box.

'Cut-lip Clip? Dad's the doctor?' Ludo enquired, peering at me under his curls.

'Yes.'

'I'd say that's one you owe me, well?'

'Oh – yes! Thank you, Ludo...'

'No thanks. Can you read?'

'Read?'

'And write?'

'...Yes?'

'I don't like to read, myself.'

'No. Don't you...' (I couldn't think.) 'It can be...'

'What?'

'Time-consuming?'

'That's right exactly!' he laughed. 'It can be time-consuming. And I've got none to consume if I'm to make up that boast just now, well?'

'Boast?'

'King of Old Pembroke Town,' he said, solemnly, and now he came close. 'I mean to do it in five.'

'Five?'

'Years.'

It barely took him two.

'Best get that box safe away, isn't it? Here. I'll carry, you show the way.'

The box was plucked from my arms.

'Vaccine you said, Clip?'

'Yes, Ludo.'

'Useful stuff...'

Swansea was tough, they're wild there. Afterwards London and Newcastle and even Liverpool were easy, because who controlled the approaches controlled all, and we had the west. But Swansea was tough. Ludo outflanked them, taking the unions and the gangs and through them the ports and through them all the power in Newport first, then Cardiff. 'Honest wages for honest work!' was our slogan, with a wink, for less than half of the work, strictly speaking, was honest.

Yes, yes, we were smugglers, bootleggers, brigands, black marketeers, profiteers, buccaneers, pirates. We were gangsters. We were a tough bunch, a bad lot, but we had heart, you know. No women, no kids – we kept the old law. And we weren't dishonest, except where the law was concerned. We had a kind of conscience. We weren't the first underground to offer services in return for service. You couldn't count the money we put into schools, clinics, soup kitchens: things the impoverished and corrupted government would not offer or could not maintain. We regulated the petty criminals and adjudicated disputes judiciously. Sign up with us and we looked after you. Fight us and you would get more fight than you could handle. We never killed except when we were forced to – but the Swansea gang, the Gweilch, wouldn't have any of it. They promised us blood.

'They're frightened,' Ludo said, sadly. 'They don't mean it.'

They had reason to be frightened, after what we did to Birmingham (dosed their drinking water, dear me – the effects wore off after a week but it was no fun while it lasted) and they did surely mean it.

'A chance to climb down with honour is all they need,' he said, but we couldn't see the chance until we heard about the wedding. One of their sea runners, Hook, a thin-faced man and cunning, was to be married. Hook had a thing going with the Bretons in Saint Malo; his boats weaved between the patrols. He paid off the Excise men and more importantly someone who told him where gaps would appear between drones. Hook's wedding would float on French champagne. All the best families in the Gweilch would be there. Some of us thought we should just blow them up.

'Never,' said Ludo, 'That would mean nine generations of war. But we ought to send some sort of present.'

We got the munition from the base at Brawdy – Ludo ran the labour there as he did the ranges at Castlemartin, the barracks at Brecon and the base at Sennybridge. Even after the Invaders came, we never lost our grip on them, which made a difference to the struggle.

The timing was exquisite, had to be. We bought one of their bouncers and had him plant the tracker. Jenks the Donkey Drop, Ludo's maths man, did the calculations. A flying-boat at such and such a height, at such a speed, dropping a package of such a weight, into a thirty-second window... Hitting the spot wasn't the problem, the laser would do that for you: it was all about the angle. Don't ask me to explain it.

Jenks had a feeling for angles that would have dumbed a computer.

Anyway, the feast was done, the space was cleared, and Hooky and his bride about to take their turn – the band raised their bows and gathered their blowing breaths – when Ludo's present arrived, smashing through the roof and the ceiling, burying itself nose-first in the centre of the floor. Picture the poor Gweilch as the dust cleared and they saw the tail fins and the prop still turning on the end of that silver cigar! There's a foot of it moled into the concrete and five more gleaming above. But instead of blowing out the building, the block and everyone, the cigar splits open and spills the dance floor with a rattling spray of hardened light. Wonder enough – but then the room fills with a recording of Ludo's boom.

'This is a love bomb for you boys – we apologise for alarming the ladies. Congratulations, Mr Hook and Charlotte! We wish you health and happiness and hope we will always stand together. Now, please, forgive our intrusion – and dance, if we be friends...'

After a few moments Hooky laughed, then they all laughed, the band struck up and Hook and Charlotte took the floor, diamonds scattering around their feet. A whole bucketful, a bombful of diamonds – that is how Ludo bought the loyalty of the Gweilch. Well, that and the face of death. It was a grand party, we heard.

It was not the last time Ludo used combinations of terror, relief and awe to master an audience and realise his will.

'Those Jacobeans had the stuff!' he exclaimed, after becoming acquainted with Webster and his Duchess. He became quite a student of the classics. I made recordings for him, readings of books I felt might interest him, as well as others I thought he ought to know. In the time of our ascendancy (when we took over the Gweilch we were living in the great house at Dinefwr) as in our time underground he would often retire to his quarters – be it the King's postered bedroom or his portion of a cave – with my voice and the words of the immortals. I started with the obvious: Macchiavelli's *Prince*, Sun Tzu's *Arts of War*, Foot's biography of Aneurin Bevan – and then we went through Shakespeare. There was never any suggestion, of course, that he could not read. It was understood that he needed to use the time working and could listen to me with one ear.

Why didn't I teach him to read? Bless you for asking! I guess you never sinned so low as to sit at the right hand of a bandit baron as he made his play for the regency. 'A' as in 'ace', 'aa' as in 'apple'. 'B', 'bu', as in bullet through the back of the neck... Revealing anything short of infallibility would not have done at all.

'You do a fair Porter, Clip,' he laughed once, 'but your Macbeth isn't black enough and Henry doesn't convince like your Fluellen!'

He came to love a good bout of literary criticism. In the first year of the war we were lying in a thicket somewhere near Bwlch one gut-wet night – it was more of a thinnet, actually, as I recall – in ambush, passing the wait for a convoy of Invaders in debate over Hamlet.

'He was a damn weak boy,' Ludo insisted, wiping the rain off his nose. 'The ghost tells him all he needs to know. There's no arguing with your father's blood – I'd have been straight down off those battlements, spit Claudius and take the crown. Polonius and his whelp would have jumped into line – grateful if I didn't do them too!'

I was trying to keep the rain out of the mortar tubes. 'But suppose the ghost is lying,' I retorted. 'A damned spirit, a devil. You wouldn't act without proof and damn yourself.'

'You don't need proof when you hear truth,' Ludo said, taking a swig from the flask and passing it over my head. (They used to nip a bit of warm on ambush, not enough to spoil the aim, just sufficient to counter the riddles of rain down the neck.) 'Look at old Othello. He gets his proof, much good does it do him.'

'You're talking about instinct. It's not a strawberry hanky he chokes her with, it's perverted instinct. We can't act on that – we need reason.'

'Reason!' Ludo roared, prompting a chorus of

shushing from the bushes where his fighters lay. He ignored them. 'Is it reason brings you out on a no-moon night in bloody February under dogbelly cloud to throw bombs at a bunch of conscripts from Guangzhou or wherever?'

'Yes,' I stubborned. 'Well, it's no bloody ghost, anyroad.'

'Isn't it, Clip?' And he smiled that smile, the same I saw the night of the Piranhas, the smile that said he had won and the earth was on its rightful axis. 'For a reader your history is thin. See down there? The Gaer? That was a Roman fort. Don't you think your ancestors lay just here, waiting to scrag a legionary or two, on a brother night to this bitch? Does history proceed by instinct or reason, Clip? The ghosts are with us tonight, mun. Be sure of it – and shoot straighter!'

Pretty well everyone heard that. If half the Liberation Army had come up the road then we would have bayonet-charged them. This was Ludo's genius. Not conviction – or not conviction alone, for that will undo you in the end, whatever Ludo thought –

but a coupling certainty of the depth of the moment, a feel for its roots in time, time forward and time back.

The conscripts in that convoy never would have had a prayer had not Ludo's policy been to spare as many as possible. A mine killed the first vehicle, my mortars got the last, and Freddie the Lingos was on the horn, telling them to throw down everything if they wanted to see their mothers again. Ten seconds was all we ever gave them and usually more than they needed. We were always fewer than we seemed, so if they fought we had to get very close and kill them quickly then, or all hell...

I preferred it when they were Chinese or Koreans. I know it's stupid. But if you've got to shank someone's innards out with a bayonet it's preferable he or she doesn't look too much like anyone in your family, and it's better you don't understand what they're screaming. Because anyone surrendering when his oppo decided to fight would be unlucky, we developed the All-For-One. They all gave up or they all died: that was Freddie's constant message and it didn't matter where they came from (the Invaders had many auxiliaries, pressed and mercenary): those who served their tours in old Britain soon knew the rule of All-For-One. The Invaders' answer to it was to court marshall anyone who came back from a fight without his weapon. The conscripts' solution, in turn, was to desert. Some headed for the towns and scrounged, other bands of them lived rough, preying on sheep and freezing. The farmers didn't like that but they knew free labour when they saw it.

We took their guns, set them to run down the valley, torched what we couldn't carry and were gone, a file of foot-knights vanishing into the black. We used to wrap ourselves in silver bags like they give victims of hypothermia – Mylar, wonderful stuff. In the beginning the drones still saw with thermal cameras; mummied up in the bags we showed no heat. Later they sent smaller, clever drones in swarms, and those things listened. They could hear your heart beat. They were terrible. It was one of them got Ninnian, Ludo's youngest brother. There weren't even bits to bury. A funeral in those days was a circle of us trying not to look over our shoulders, with a bit of a bag in a hole if you were lucky, and all of us crying as the bag leaked red.

Well, that ambush was near the beginning of the war. Before we knew how wars go, the beginning was – awful to think – but it was a heady time. A time to be alive! 'Peacekeeping', they called it, as they bombed us, shelled us, rocketed us, mined us – and for every fighter they killed twelve innocents. The old UN was their beaten dog and in the name of something called 'International Opinion' it was decreed that invisible things called 'the Worldwide Financial System' and 'the Stability of the ICU' required the 'emergency development' of 'failed states' – it was all dressed up marvellous in fancy language.

We scorned them.

'Cheeky buggers!' Ludo was quoted as saying. 'There's nothing failed about this state. We know what they want. They can well afford our water-prices but they're fixing for smash and grab.'

All sorts of people streamed to us. Ludo ordered a welcome in the hillsides for Moroccans, French, Romanians, Touaregs, Libyans, English, Italians, you name it – mostly their young, their passionate and of course their Believers came. The Invaders hated the Believers, called them the Poison of Democracy, said they raised havoc wherever they went. We took the opposite view: believe what you want. Until the peace Ludo never really troubled over anyone else's faith – but I'm running ahead again. The fact was, anyone who didn't fancy being chipped and coded came west and we took them in. Many became our recruits. It wasn't the first time, as the scholars pointed out. Didn't the old Blue People hide here from the Romans, and fight a twenty-five-year guerrilla war against them?

The European Government could see the way it was going to go but they were petrified by implications. They sent Ludo ambassadors, offering all sorts of amnesties and absolutions if he would only fall into line: as well as the Believers, the Invaders were now using Ludo as their primary excuse.

'If you won't stand up I can't back you,' was Ludo's reply, accompanied by whispered advice to appoint him Defence Minister of the Union as quickly as possible. But of course they didn't and that was that. Space-based missile systems, bach! Motions, votes and resolutions come up rather short against them. The ships and planes, the armour and the guns of old Europe were specked to hot scrap in a day. The European Governing Council never quite got round to giving the order to fire back.

We were 'fundamentalists', because some of us still believed in God. We were 'hill-niggers'; we were 'two-pound Taliban' because if you fought for Ludo he paid you enough for a fish supper. And they installed an Interim Government of sell-outs and blacklegs, people who took baths in all the ICUs they shipped in, wrapped in polythene: great slabs of coloured paper which were supposed to make us forget the centuries we had lived as free people. And they arranged 'elections' in which you could vote for this stooge or that traitor, and why wouldn't we accept it? And they put out 'Wanted' lists and offered fortunes to anyone who would turn us in. And they hunted us like rats.

But rats is hard killing, especially when they wise up to the traps. First we got rid of phones and computers, then the radios, then pretty well everything with a battery. We co-ordinated our fight through boys on scrambling bikes carrying handwritten notes. As you can imagine, that called for a pretty high degree of devolution among the different commanders, but it worked well. Busy times! It didn't take long for the Invaders to identify my script.

'Look Clip! They want you almost as much as me!' Ludo said. 'For that much it's worth turning yourself in!'

A million ICUs on your head don't make for the softest pillow, but then pillows weren't much of our equipment. We moved fast and light, from hillside caves to hedges, ditches, woods and old mineshafts. We spent five months underground once, near Blaenavon. There's little enough to recommend the troglodyte life except it's harder for the drones to follow you. The ones the size of tea cups with just enough explosive to jelly a roomful of you; thermobaric warheads: a curse on whoever came up with them. They killed our families, our friends, our children – shot, bombed and blasted. We wept rage but we wouldn't quit. And we had our revenges too. Blew up the puppet governor of Glamorgan, and Crian sniped the collaborator finance minister – the best shot fired in Wales since the invention of gunpowder... bless that girl, she was a genius with a rifle.

Pick of the pops, we brought down that helicopter with two members of their Praesidium inside, on their way to what they thought was a secret council inside Cardiff Castle. Nothing the Tourist Board could say would persuade their top nobs to visit Wales after that. Half the old British Army had done their training on our hills so many who joined us knew the ground we fought on. And what a grand country is Wales for guerilla war! Dimpled and rippled with ruins and wrinkles, furrowed with stream-cuts, rumpled with folded hills. Show me any view in Wales and I'll show you double a dozen pockets where you can hide a platoon.

And we – I – read all the classic texts. Castro, Trotsky, Che, Ho Chi Minh. There's enough ammo on half a library shelf to bring down any tyrant – remember that, though I hope you never need it. Do you still have libraries, I wonder? Or books, even? Hang on to whatever's left, is my advice. Screens are all very fine (if you don't mind them knowing what you read, controlling what you can get and knowing when and where you read it) but they would have been death to us. I read all those histories to Ludo while he got on with directing his own version. People said he was the heir to Glyndwr and Llewellyn but he was more successful than either of them.

The second year of the war was vicious and the third turned even worse. Llandovery was a marvellous piece of organisation. March, and a bitter one, another no-moon night. (We recruited the silver girl as a terror weapon – those poor conscripts. Monthly, when she looked away, they knew we'd come for them somewhere.) Thirty of us moved into

Llandovery and went door to door. We'd indentified certain competent people in the town who could be roused and then set to rouse others, according to a list. Once out of their houses the population was directed along a certain road, up a hill and into a wood. (It took an hour longer than I had planned because of the dogs, cats, rabbits and bloody budgies. People said they would either bring the pets or stay home with them, so the budgies came too.)

Just before the light, ten miles away, a team set off the charges in the wall of the dam of Llyn Brianne. Waters that had been penned a hundred storeys high ran wild again, for the first time since the dam was built back in 1972. God, the noise! I thought they had overcooked it and blown the lid off hell. And then there was a thing like a silver-black dragon, exploding elemental out of the valley. Torrents came down like God's vast vengeance and that was the end of the garrison, and the better part of Llandovery.

We'd stuffed the wood with stores, tents, cooking equipment, fuel and sleeping bags. We apologised for wrecking the homes, schools and shops which the waters had washed away and promised fulsome compensation for the whole town when the war was over.

'And when's that going to be?' they cried.

'Much sooner than you think, friends,' we said.

When frowning dawn came up on the Towy valley five hundred young men and women were rolling over the flooded meadows with their uniforms painted in red mud and eyes that did not blink the rain. The old crows were bloody yodelling.

The Invaders always tried to hide their bad news (you still won't find any of this in their histories) but even they couldn't bury those corpses. How had we done it? How did we blind the satellites and their UAVs? Clearly it wasn't staged to turn opinion against us, though they'd rather that was believed than the truth! And we had no mole in their high command, though they tortured dozens of their own people to be sure. No, no. Levello we had to thank for it. Levello gave us our secret weapon: Theo the Bug.

Long thin fingers like a bug's legs, poppy eyes like a bug's eyes and speaking Bulgarian which sounded to me like a bug's language, bless him – but none of that gave him his name, or not entirely, anyway. Theo the Bug had studied at the University of the Atlantic in St Donat's when he and the world were young. I've no idea how Levello got hold of him. None of us even knew he existed. We were more concerned with Uzma when we set up the meeting, the first parliament, but there – I've run ahead again.

December in the second year of the war and the resistance was but beat. No one would help us: too frightened. We were living like water rats in holts around Tregaron and Newcastle Emlyn. The holts were a piece of genius; the idea came from beavers and otters, it was a Canadian, MacInnis, who thought of it. A wonderful engineer he was. 'Use the water!' said MacInnis.

'The drones can't fly through it, the cameras can't see through it – and it's everywhere,' as he said. He taught us to dig chambers in the river banks and reservoirs so that the entrance tunnels were below the lowest water level: easy in winter. We tunnelled up into the dry, or dryish, and that's where we lived. If they found one the poor buggers inside wouldn't know a thing about it: a bunker-buster and no survivors. And then there were their Special Forces, crawling about in culverts and burying themselves under bracken. They never surrendered, I'll give them that. We caught six dug into a cemetery near Cefn Coed, up above Merthyr. It began as a great scrap but it set off terrible things, the worst of the war.

The whole of Merthyr was a designated Insurgent Zone, along with Pontypridd and everything from Aberdare to Rhymney, all the way to the Vale of Neath. Those people! The greatest of the great: Ludo always said that if it wasn't for the Invaders his writ would never have run to the Valleys, but once they arrived that was it. The Valley Boys and Valley Girls came over to us wholesale and the Invaders could barely buy one of them – they would rather take the wheels off APCs in the middle of Merthyr in broad daylight and flog them down the pub than claim a cent of traitor's treasure. So the Invaders set up their observation posts on the flanks of hills above, aiming to catch fighters on their ways in or out, and anyone without a movement pass. They had drones circling over those valleys like clouds of rooks. We moved with great circumspection.

One day we were over at Penderyn talking to the distillers there about making up a special whisky for delivery to the forts (we knew how much some of their officers liked a drink, and wouldn't you, so far from home?) when this boy, Phil the Fly they called him, Lord knows why, comes panting in – not the fittest, he'd only come down from the pub – and says there's a nest of Specials in the cemetery at Cefn Coed. Ludo decides we'll get them because they liked to pretend their Specials were invulnerable, invisible, and we wanted to show them and the valley that such was not the case. So we arrange a funeral, a hearse with a coffin full of guns, mourners with flak jackets under their macs, the lot, and cloned movement passes for everyone of course, and at dusk two days later we go in.

Three of the Specials were hit straight off. One died but the rest – including the wounded – fought. They called in their missiles and bombs, we closed with them and the dead were fairly jumping out of their graves in that cemetery, no exaggeration. Ludo had rocket teams waiting for the helicopters and when they came we got two. But all the excitement was too much for Merthyr. The Invaders had one garrison in the Castle Hotel in town, and another in Cyfarthfa Castle itself. (There wasn't a castle in all of Wales without a detachment of the Liberation Army in residence by this time – don't imagine we missed the irony.) Anyway, with no plan, no insiders and no whisper of plot beforehand, Merthyr rose against the Invaders. History will tell you about the first Merthyr Rising against the Ironmasters and the English – well, this was the second.

They didn't wait for us, either. They knew where our caches were so they broke them open and in they went. It should have been suicide. At Cyfarthfa it was, but they had better luck at the hotel. By the time the helicopters arrived to rescue the garrison that garrison were all dead and the boys had taken over the heavy weapons. The Invaders lost two more helicopters before they decided to settle for bombing the town to shards. Most people fled as soon as it kicked off, but it got worse two days later when they sent a column up from Cardiff to relieve the castle. That was how Merthyr was flattened. They never published casualty figures but anyone who had gone back died, as well as anyone who was still there.

'What happened in Merthyr' – you heard the phrase years after, like a curse that wouldn't be lifted. And it wasn't just Merthyr. The tanks shelled 'insurgent strongholds' all the way up the Taff. Ponty, Aberfan: it was reprisal and it changed the war. The tides of exhilaration at the Rising, then the anger and despair at the aftermath and the feeling that you couldn't touch them without bringing down monsoons of d-uranium rain... it changed everything.

'What can we do?' people said. 'They can hear our thoughts. No one can say anything; if the wind can catch it they hear it; if we rise they kill us all. What can we do?'

Little Mari Evans from Bridgend was the first to answer. Seventeen years old. God knows where she got the stuff. Blue Mari they called her, she dyed her hair. She was the first. At the station, when troops were coming in and another regiment was rotating out. She picked her time perfectly, Blue Mari, and took twenty-six of them with her. There were two days of death-quiet then, while the Invaders crammed the sky with drones. So many! They were the only sound, like little tractors ploughing the clouds. They said you could walk in the rain and their wings would keep you dry. And then it seemed to take, like fire.

Our people and our children blew themselves up, scattered themselves away like seeds on the care-nothing wind. We couldn't bear it, for all that they killed our foes. Ludo put out an appeal for it to stop but it only seemed to make it worse. Like a plague on both your houses – another bomb, or three bombs, every day. The Invaders were terrified. Shot down scores of innocents in case they weren't. And we felt we had nowhere to turn, then. How could we stop? We'd started it all – and there were those among us who thought nothing of slipping the suicides a pack of this or that: you just strap it on, so, and press here... The bomb kids didn't seem to be able to stop: too much ecstasy and too much despair. So the only way to stop it was to win it, to drive the Invaders out. But how? How, in hell?

We considered desperate things. Blow the power stations, some said. Let's make a nuclear desert if that's the only way to break their grip. Ludo wouldn't have it: 'They'll be the masters of the desert,' he said.

'Poison the reservoirs?'

'No,' he said, 'who's to say when the waters clear that their flag won't still be flying?'

The solution he came up with was as grand and mad as he was then: 'We'll have to widen it,' he said. 'Fires from here to Vladi-bloody-vostok. Our enemy is a calculator. We force his calculations until he scats. We need to turn his face, like Napoleon or

Hitler. Another Russia's what we want! Another...'

We thought of Uzma.

Uzma! Difficult to separate the girl you were from the icon you became. You were a craze to them, to the screaming legions. Not so bad to begin with: it wasn't your fault you made everyone jealous, all the time. But later, when your favour ennobled them and your mere name inspired crazy dreams – you near cleaved us in half. You certainly cleaved me.

Going back, anyway. You were the only child of the ruling dynasty of the mightiest port of all – Karachi. We first heard of you before the war when Levello appeared one day, eyes widened by what he'd seen and had to say of you. You were marriageable age, famously beautiful and famously rejecting. Your dowry was half the subcontinent. Ludo now was the Bandit King of the West: just, acknowledged and revered. The Invaders were far away, still, wrapping up the remnants of the Americas and striking their infamous treaty with India. Africa was a plum in their maw, a continent transformed into an opencast mine, a stagger of dams and a million market gardens. Only Pakistan and Europe were still free.

Levello came to Ludo and they held one of their brotherly summits, at the Bear in Crickhowell. Even before the misunderstanding they understood one another best when they were both under a butt of sack. I got a call around three in the morning – would I please go down to the dining hall? The two of them were aflame with drink. Ludo roared as I walked in.

'Ah – here now! Here's Clip! Here's my mun!'

All his barons and baronesses, the whole royal underworld of Wales banged their jealous fists on the long table, ululating ersatz affection.

'My brother here has come to ask for my blessing on his marriage!'

Now Levello's people put up their bay of cheers.

'What do you say to that, clever Clip?'

'Who is the lucky lady?'

'Who indeed!' cried Ludo. 'Who but the star of the East herself, the prettiest woman beyond the Severn?'

'Who?'

'Uzma Khan,' said dark Levello, and the room was silence. They'd had the discussion between them. As ever, Ludo was using me as his mouthpiece and sounding board.

'Uzma Khan,' I said.

'Herself,' Levello confirmed.

'And why Uzma?' Ludo rhetoricked.

'Because I bloody love her, and because our peoples will have the run of the world. See!' Levello shouted, and the wall behind him lit up and there she was, on a webcam, smiling and chewing gum. She looked like a teenage gangster queen until she took her sunglasses off, shot us a smile, whipped the gum out and raised her chin to us. Then she was just a queen.

'My heart's congratulations!' I shouted, a bit squeaky, because in only that time I'd felt trouble. 'Blessings on you, Levello. And blessings on your beautiful bride!'

And then all in the room were on their feet and cheering and Ludo, over the top of a foaming pint, tipped me a right rogue's wink.

'Brother,' he said, when he'd swallowed the toast, 'Clip puts it well. You have all our blessings. Will I be your best man?'

Over in Karachi the news of Levello's intentions was not so simply received. They held a meeting to discuss our proposal, recorded by Ludo but written by me, that their pearl of a girl and his brother should be married forthwith. For all that it would be a good match, the mighty brothers and the mighty Khans, their problem was plain: Levello, in their terms, was a godless heathen, or possibly a pagan; in any case an infidel. We waited for this objection, which duly came, and then we played our ace.

Levello would convert. Why not? How hard is it to say 'There is no God but God' (self-evident, if you accept the premise) and 'Muhammad is his Prophet'? Of course Muhammad, peace be upon him, was his prophet! So Levello said it and said it well and Pakistan rejoiced. While some in Wales wondered what sort of Muslim he'd make everyone else was on to nattering about the wedding. What was being wedded was both so extraordinary and ordinary that few seemed to give it much thought, at least in public.

The wedding was a double triumph, with part one celebrated in Karachi. Then Uzma and her prince took ship for Wales. Here they processed through the country, from Newport docks where they landed to St David's (where they married a second time), to Caernarvon Castle where they honeymooned – and the nation fell for her. Old boys wouldn't shut up about what a lovely girl she was; young men dreamed their longing dreams and the women copied her clothes and hair. I realised the size of it one day in a chippy in Cardigan. The three old girls behind the counter were white as cod, grey roots showing under dyed black hair, and their dugs half fell out of their saris. Well, well.

And then came the Invaders, and the war, and Levello and Uzma had to quit their royal quarters and go underground. Before all that, in the so-called happy time, I met her at the wedding part two, on a high summer day in St David's. She figured I'd written Ludo's recitation and sought me out to thank me. It was an open-air banquet in the Bishop's Palace. A cool brown hand on my arm and I looked up, into those eyes. High behind her a cloud of jackdaws burst like black fireworks.

'Thank you, Clip,' she says, 'that was so beautiful.'

'My queen,' I stammered.

'Am I?' she grinned. She must have been in her twenties then but she had all the chirrup of a teenager, the princess with the street smarts.

'On my life,' I said.

'Thank you,' she said, 'you beautiful thing,' and she kissed my gam-split mouth. I watched her ankles, with their bracelets, walk away.

'Uzma,' Ludo said. 'Her people. We fire them up and it's bloody Jihad! Let's see the Invader cost-benefit a spot of holy war!'

I tried to dissuade him, of course.

'You light that lamp,' I said, 'and there'll be

nowhere for the rest of us to hide. God knows our opponents are numerous now, why multiply them? We're infidels, remember?'

'We'll convert,' said Ludo. 'Easy.'

'Get on! Can you see them in the Red Lion? Drinking lemon soda and puffing apple pipes? A bit of hubbly bubbly with that, bach? No, I'm sorry, we seem to be fresh out of scratchings... What about the trade? Know how much we make off bootleg and smuggle? What about the women? What about the gays, come to that?'

'The women all wear the costume already!'

'Because they choose to,' I raved. 'Because they think it fun and pretty. It's fashion! You're going to tell them to cover their heads? Their arms? Their butt-cracks? Have you seen the version of modest Muslim dress now prevailing in Porthcawl? You'll get a holy war. We'll be lynched.'

'There're Muslims and Muslims,' Ludo said. 'Haven't these islands converted once already? Augustine of Canterbury did it. We can do it. And then fat Henry adapted it to local conditions as they suited. Pack your make-up bag! We're going to see my brother and my sister-in-law.'

So we went north. Moose and Roger le Gallois, Ludo's bodyguards, and the gorgeous Crian, Ludo's boon companion, who could hit a wasp with a rifle shot at half a mile, and me, his Pen, went north together, to Snowdonia, in the middle of winter. We slept at hill farms and in tumbling barns and we walked and walked, driving a flock before us. Droving made good camouflage because the Invaders knew no shepherding: they left it to the Ethiopians to raise their flocks. It didn't seem strange to them to be moving sheep in the dead of winter (and to think sheep came out of Asia). Up the bare spine we journeyed, through the harshest country.

Moose and Roger le Gallois saved me: they were two funny big men, for all their kills, and they kept up a banter across days of iron ground and hillsides of frozen screes. It was so cold you thought your teeth would crack. Though he sometimes smiled at their comedy, Ludo was mostly silent, mulling over the composition of his next costume, Augustine's habit under the doublet of Henry VIII. In the resting times I read to the company from the Holy Koran. When we came to move on, Roger le Gallois would rouse us with his version of the call to prayer: 'Aaaaaaaaright Butt!' was the first line, then, aimed at Moose, came the second: 'Geeeeet-UP Mun!'

We had no way of warning Levello of our purposes. Ludo and his strategist, his best shot and two of his greatest warriors, driving three hundred sheep – it would worry anyone. Sheep, as everyone knows, can mean all kinds of things. When we had to move arms or explosives we often used sheep. Tie the stuff under them and they'll carry it under the noses of the drones. If you want to rout a camp, a few suicide sheep – one of Roger's specialities – with a bit of a bang bound by every belly can raise a bleating hell.

So, hearing of the advance of our little flotilla, and ignorant of our intentions, Levello came out to meet us. Remember, this was a cruel time. The ICUs of the Invaders, and their terrible power of hearing, had scored and scarred our people. There were betrayers among us now. Towns and villages, even families had been split and sold. Perhaps Levello's more paranoid advisers might be forgiven their fears. At any rate, Levello came out with a small armada of fighters. We met in a short sea of mountain-moor south of Machynlleth. We had had horses for a day or so now, and were riding down, sun low behind us, when we perceived Levello's band coming up out of the trough.

No word passed but Crian's rifle was out and Roger le Gallois and Moose had split left and right like hunting dogs, ready to circle the flanks. The size and aspect of the other party had barely registered with me before the snick and rattle of weapons told they were ready for the reddening, at his signal.

'Wait up,' said Ludo, 'it's my brother, isn't it?'

'And too many friends,' Moose answered. 'Say we cut the odds?'

'You take the twenty-seven on the right...' suggested Roger le Gallois, and his smile did not entirely undercut the offer. Crian was looking through her telescopic sight. 'They've drawn,' she said.

'All of you hold,' Ludo instructed. 'I will go down and talk to Levello. And keep those bloody sheep back, will you?'

Roger whistled and the dog Apollo was off like a black lasso round the flock. Ludo threw his rifle to me and set off down the hill.

Now followed a bad couple of minutes while he drew closer to them and Levello's band did not at first pause, but then hesitated, like a cat high on its toes. Now they stopped too, save a solitary rider who pushed his horse on.

'Levello,' said Crian, 'He's... shall we give all the West to his brother?'

'Only if you're ready to do Ludo with the second shot,' I said. 'Put it up.'

She didn't. Down below the brothers drew closer, closer, and met. At first they leaned together, embracing across the gap between their horses.

'All friends,' said Crian, still peering. We watched as the redhead and the dark settled back in their saddles to talk. And talk. Minute after long minute we sat there, hunched in shiver, as the parley continued.

'What are they doing down there,' Moose grumbled, 'bloody Sudoku?'

His restiveness echoed in Levello's followers. Their horses circled and stamped uneasy. Night was close, the sun swallowed in a front, hag-black, where a storm came on.

'Not good,' Crian said, suddenly, and her right hand blurred, jacking a cartridge into the breech.

Roger le Gallois pursed his lips. 'You've never seen a wasp. At this time of year?'

'They're arguing,' she said, 'look.'

Ludo was forward in his saddle, his arm making some angry point, and Levello's gestures were abrupt, insulted, throwing aside whatever was being presented. Now the sound of their voices reached us through the frigid air, hard as ravens' grievance. I swung binoculars back to Levello's group. If it went to shooting I would spot for Crian. If they had anyone half as good as her I wouldn't last ninety seconds.

'What are the others doing?' she murmured. Her sights were still on her lover's brother. If he raised his hand to Ludo she'd shoot him before he'd shaped the blow.

'Levello's lot? Same as us. Watching.'

'Tell me if they raise their hackles. Have they got a shooter?'

'Oh aye,' said Roger, 'Sheepfold at 11 o'clock? He went down by the wall there, to the right of it, see?'

'No. No. No... yes. Got him. Hel-lo... what's that piddly little gun you've got there then... You looking at me?'

'Don't!' I cried, 'Ludo will bloody have us if we fire first. How's the family?'

Crian moved her aim back. 'Oh! Better!' she said. 'They seem to be refreshing themselves.'

'Bastards,' said Moose. 'Have we got anything left, Rog? Or did you have it all? For your nerves? When you got windy last night?'

The brothers had both produced golden bottles. Through the binoculars I watched them tilt them up and suckle like giant babies, then swap, tilt and suck again. Crian had a lovely giggle, like a fairy bell.

'She's getting merry just watching them,' Roger said. 'You watch her now, she'll start potting grasshoppers and singing.'

'Grasshoppers on this hill will be froze to their holes by their nuts,' Moose informed us. 'What's so funny girl?'

'Those two,' she said, 'God they can drink! Levello must have struck some deal with Allah.'

'Or it's cold tea,' said Roger.

Now their laughter reached us and we could see they had changed. Their gestures were quite different, as if they were tossing jokes between them.

'We can't wait anymore,' I said. 'One bloody drone and it's war over. Get the sheep moving, we're going down.'

'Don't you go near those sheep,' Roger said, 'you'll frighten them out of their wits. Apollo! Out by!'

'What wits? They're bloody sheep,' Moose objected.

'More wits than ewe!'

'No guns now,' I said. We sheathed and rode down to join our masters. Ludo waved us on and Levello signalled his troop, who turned their beasts towards the valley. And so in procession we nodded down off the hills and rode towards Machynlleth.

We could not make elaborate plans: who was there and where we happened to be was all that ordained our meetings. The University of Technology at Machynlleth had a hall and Levello many friends among the staff and students, so that is where we went. We could not be sure that the Invaders wouldn't catch the scent of something and send a package down from the troposphere to make the place a crater: the possibility put a lick of urgency under the proceedings. Levello's people sat to the right of the aisle, Ludo's few to the left, and Ludo, as guest, was first to take the platform. He was about to speak when the doors flung open.

Uzma had a few people with her, mostly women, and there was a general reshuffle as gallants gave up their seats at the front to make way for them – she took what had been mine, beside Levello.

'Hello Clip,' she murmured, 'thank you, sweetie.'

She stretched herself in her seat and said, loudly, 'Now, what's all this, you two? Arguing about a hill?'

'There was no real argument,' Ludo smiled.

'I heard there was.'

'Well there was but then your husband realised we were somehow cursed, and proposed we wash the air...'

'With whisky.'

'With fine spirit! And then there were no more misunderstandings.'

'What were the misunderstandings?'

'Best forgotten, Uzma.'

'I would know, Ludo.'

'Well...'

'When Ludo spoke of his love for us,' Levello interrupted, 'I heard prevarication.'

'And when he asked for substance,' said Ludo, earnestly, 'I heard suspicion.'

'And his unhappiness at this presumed suspicion led him to suspect,' Levello said, 'naturally. So hearing as I thought prevarication and suspicion I was angered, and short with him, and heated, and I accused.'

'My accusations soon answered his,' Ludo confessed, looking embarrassed. 'And one or two old things came up, from when we were kids.'

'Yeah,' said Levello, and stopped himself.

'And?' Uzma raised her brows at her husband.

'Then I realised a curse had come between us and thought of ways to break it.'

'Hence the whisky.'

'Hence, as you put it. Indeed.'

'Nice one darling. So what's now?'

She let Levello squeeze her hand and they both turned, expectant, to the rostrum and Ludo. He was well gathered now, and launched into it.

'Brother, sister, friends. Believe I would not intrude on you, uninvited, without cause. But since what happened in Merthyr, and what with the bomb children, it seems to us that we have fallen into a winter with no hope of spring. We cannot beat our oppressors easily or soon. We cannot stop fighting them, for their victory would be the triumph of wrong, the leavening of our nation, the breaking of our people and our own great lasting shame. Nor can we continue in the hope of someday fulfilment, because the interest on this mortgaged time is paid daily in blood by desperate innocents. I believe that our hope lies in a shorter, wider struggle. I propose we fan resistance in the hearts of good men and women beyond these islands; I propose we make half the world they rule ungovernable to these rapacious and cold-souled Invaders; I propose to set fires under all their enterprises from here to Kandahar. We are outnumbered and overmatched. We must multiply the stakes and make this game they play with us unendurable, so that they will end it.'

He paused.

'How?' Uzma asked.

'Holy war,' said Ludo.

'I knew it!' she exclaimed, and not in a courtly way. 'Ludo!' she cried, 'my people are not fools! They will take one semi-hollow Muslim – they know he's a great man and a good one really – but you won't sell them a whole nation. Not unless you mean it. No less than the Invaders they will see your strategy. Can you not think of a better solution to the fire in your house than that you should burn your neighbour's?'

'I will accept Allah as my Lord if He will accept me. I will lead this nation to Him only hoping for His mercy and that He will help us.'

'But your people have their own Book, little though they read it! Two thousand years and more – what are you going to do with them?'

'In my father's house there are many mansions, Christ said.'

'And no one comes to the father except through me!' Uzma retorted.

Ludo smiled that smile, but gently. 'Indeed. We have come through him. Perhaps this is where he has led us!'

Moose, who was sitting next to me, was one of many who rumbled then. 'This mean I can have three wives or what?'

But now Levello leapt up to the stage and covered

the microphone with one hand and whispered in his brother's ear.

Ludo said, 'You what?'

Levello nodded emphatically and leaned and whispered again. After a minute Ludo recoiled slightly, amazement and calculation fighting in his eyes. Then he broke a great strange grin. He gently removed his brother's hand from the microphone, paused, looking at the floor (the first time I ever saw him search for words) then raised his head and spoke.

'Uzma. This is... remarkable. It seems my brother has another idea, and now I must answer for mine.'

He turned and strode to his pack. He returned, holding a familiar bottle. He wrenched its cork out with his teeth and blew it away like a fat pellet.

'I believe it is the duty of Muslims to spread the word of God,' Ludo said, in a solemn tone, though with a something disbelieving grin. 'But on my life I never will force any man, woman or child to follow me where I go now. For me, and with all my heart, there is no God but God, and Muhammad – Peace be Upon Him – Muhammad is His Prophet!'

And with that he upended the golden bottle, holding it high, and let the contents pour, splattering the stage. And the Muslims in the hall jumped up and shouted praise to God, and those of us who were not Muslims, perceiving that something (however bizarre to us, yet wonderful to him) had happened to our Lord, who at that moment was never less our Lord nor more a simple man – we raised our voices too, and shouted our salutes.

'If I'd only known he was going to do that...' Moose said, shaking his head at the fuming puddle, though he was smiling. And perhaps Ludo might have understood the sentiment, but not then nor ever after did he bend, backtrack or let on. For in between offering to become a Muslim and becoming one, a miracle, as he saw it, had happened, and Ludo – never a man to ignore a sign or deny a moment its deserts – had chosen the name by which he would bless it and give thanks.

'Do you think he's confusing Islam with taking the Pledge?' Roger le Gallois asked me later. 'And if he is, shouldn't someone tell him?'

We were settled in sleeping bags in a tepee somewhere in the rocky dark higher up the valley. There was a little encampment of tepees there, owned by the university. By this time I had had a few words with Ludo and had been appraised, in frustratingly vague outline, of what Levello had proposed. My head was still spinning with that, and Ludo's conversion.

'He means it,' I said, staring into the embers of a fire.

'He's going to start reading the Koran, and stop shaving, and make a pilgrimage to Mecca?'

'Well,' I smiled, 'I don't know if he'll tick all the boxes. But he's on his way, that's certain. Notice I'm not reading to him tonight.'

'Little Crian?'

'Aye. And she's a Muslim, her family came from Somalia.'

'Well, well.'

'Mmm.'

Roger said something quietly, almost to himself.

'What was that?'

'Can stars trace new tracks?'

There were many rumours about that trip. We'd all had some mystical experience. We'd seen things. We'd struck a deal with the White Goddess, or the red devil himself. All nonsense. It happened as I have described, and the next day we met Theo the Bug. Levello had him all set up in one of his summer places.

Those hills, the Rhinnogs, you ever been up there? There's nothing. A lot of old rocks and one or two ruins, hell in the winter. But Levello had a place in a high valley. It took most of the day to reach it up stream beds, through angry woods and past any number of pickets. I must have missed a lot of them but what I saw were enough to stop an army. They could have riddled that old Land Rover a hundred times and we'd never have seen where it came from. The house itself had a flagstone floor like you never saw – huge, octagonal. It had been used for meetings since who knows when. There were trees growing up the stairs and most of it was shell, but they'd made bits very comfortable. Uzma was in a holiday mood, having dressed for the outing, perhaps satirically, in a full veil and thousand ICU sandals. When Levello, laughing, protested it wasn't the best gear for the Rhinnogs in February, she said: 'A girl can go out however she wants, right Clip?'

To Ludo, as he put out a hand to help her out of the Land Rover, she said: 'You approve, don't you sailor?'

All you could see were her eyes, and ankles.

'Theo!'

'Uzma! You are – in the pink!'

The burka actually was bright pink. She embraced him with an affection that made me jealous. But he was such a gentle soul, Theo, you took to him straightly. If we'd been able to tour him around the garrisons I'm sure he would have converted them to peace by his merest appearance. But they would have shot him, or more likely flown him to a room in the East and made him run their world – so, instead, he helped us break it.

'There you are,' said Levello, 'just ask Theo.'

In the cellar Theo had a great many computers, which he took us down to meet.

'Built them all to his instruction,' Levello said, proud as a new dad. They used the heat off the machines to warm the house.

'Actually where do you want to go?' Theo asked, settling into his chair. Ludo looked enormous standing over him, and a little lost.

'Where can we go?'

'Anywhere.'

'Anywhere! Well. How about Fishguard?'

'Feesh-guard,' Theo said, thoughtfully, and there we were, looking down on it. 'Where in Fishguard?'

'The barracks?'

'Barr-acks,' said Theo, as if he were practising his English.

'What's those Clip?'

A row of tuberous lumps the colour of dolphins, with a few uniforms fussing with them.

'Robot subs.'

'Those bloody things.'

'You want to do something?' Theo looked up over his shoulder at Ludo, and there was both reluctance and longing in his gentle face.

'You bloody bet. Can we?'

Theo looked at Levello now. Levello nodded. Theo's fingers rapped. 'You can do it,' he said. 'If you press Enter.'

There was a cross-hairs over the cylinders now. I'm sure we've all seen it enough times. Ludo leaned in and pressed the key firmly. A spinning reel of milli-seconds began to flash down in one corner of the screen and then there was a squirt all across it like squid ink, as if something had burst in the machine, and then you saw it was smoke, and there was a uniform skewing off, like an ant on fire, capering towards the dock. I thought it was a woman, don't ask me why. I know it was.

'Have you got any chai, Levello love?' Uzma shouted, down the stairs.

'Coming, angel!'

'Yeah – do! Don't you start playing with Theo's stuff, boys, alright? You'll be there all day.'

'Spend a lot of time down here, do you?' Ludo asked his brother.

'A bit. Since we got it running, yeah.'

'Well. When was that?'

'Christmas.'

That was the second time I saw Ludo look for words.

'What do you think?' he said, at last.

'It's heavy business,' said Levello.

'Heavy business,' echoed Theo.

I felt myself flush. Six weeks! We had been children for six weeks! Levello had drones – what else did he have? I hadn't heard a thing – and I was supposed to be Ludo's head of counter-intelligence! Uzma, I thought. Technology from Pakistan. That's a dowry.

'Where do you fly your drones from?' Ludo asked casually, as we climbed the stairs, 'Old RAF Valley?'

'I haven't got any drones!' Levello cried. 'What an accusation!'

'What? That wasn't...'

'Theirs,' said Levello.

Ludo turned around slowly and looked at Theo.

'You've – broken their codes?'

Theo wobbled his head, cast a shy glance. 'Broken. Not exactly.'

'Of course he hasn't broken them, they're working fine. Apart from the odd bug. He's – administering them,' said Levello.

'He's *administering* them?' Ludo growled, like a man, like a king, actually, being set up for a pratfall. 'Well – what?'

'Theo is Systems Administrator Number Star One' Levello announced, grandly. 'Theo the Bug!'

'*Number Star One?* And that means?'

'It means that the Central Committee of the People's Federated States couldn't even get a cup of coffee if Theo decided to give their percolator a headache.'

'Is not bad system,' Theo said, as if embarrassed on behalf of whoever designed it, 'but does bad things.'

'Oh, I'd love a cup of coffee,' sighed a sofa, over the arm of which I now perceived a pair of beautiful if not rugged shoes. 'Can you show them how to do it please, Theo? They can be right dozy, these two.

Actually I'll have a chai. And will you come and read to me, lovely Clip?'

Levello offered Theo's services, on the condition that Theo offered them, and Theo did. His only request was that he might work out of his office, which was fair, of course, much as we would have loved to have taken him south. I think perhaps Levello was relieved. Oh, I know he was. Ludo was the head of the resistance and Levello knew the terrible, cursing power of the Bug as well as anyone. If he had been the kind of man to wield it we would never have made it to Machynlleth. They'd watched us on that hillside, be sure.

With the Bug our communication problems were solved. One thing I learned in war – and it holds for peace for all I know – when you haven't got communications problems you haven't got problems. Don't ask me what kind of phones Theo gave them, they looked normal to me, but Theo said they might as well be unhackable. It crossed my mind, too, that if the brothers ever did fall out then Ludo's end of the hotline would make a tasty tracker for a five-hundred-pound thermobaric signal of displeasure, but Ludo growled when I raised the point.

It was still an unfair fight. God knows how many programmers they had, and how many machines, and we had one Bulgarian who lived on sardine sandwiches, adored Uzma, had a thing for breakfast TV in Welsh (which he was learning) and also for books of philosophy.

Ludo went to pray while I read to Uzma. An old gift-edition of *The Economist* World Briefing it was, all lovely glossy paper. And not exactly ornamentally written, though still I tried to put it over as you do: romantically, engagingly, even comically, if you're reading to the most beautiful girl in your life. And then the meeting was over, the deal was struck, and we set out south again, with much news. We would not say a word about the Bug, of course, but rumours of Ludo's conversion ran wild ahead of us.

At first we feared. We feared prating bigots, homilies and holy hobnobs, endless visits to mosques, Muhammad, Peace be Upon Him, says this; Muhammad, Peace Be Upon Him, says that. Submission – *submission!* Submission was what we hated. We demanded it of those who opposed us in the beginning, yes, but they were mostly small-fish gangsters, or gangs like the Gweilch. But we said sign up to this, our way's the way, then carry on: we'll all be stronger for it. We didn't want to pay knee-service to some dusty ideology in which there was no room for our pleasures, which regarded pleasure itself as sin. So we kept a wary eye on Ludo, lest he yaw towards something we felt sure he was not, and could not and should not be. We loved him and followed him because he espoused no higher law than the freedom and benefit of his people. If he was going to go setting something higher than that, well, people were going to have things to say about it.

It took a while to see our fears unfounded. My own were petty. I was jealous of Crian and his other teachers, who were mostly like her, beautiful Muslim women. I read the Koran like fury, over and again, so that I might retain my place at the heart of Ludo's mind. But I did them a disservice, Crian and Mizbah, and Ludo too. I should have trusted in his innate sense of disputation, especially when it came to texts.

'A God of conscience is my God,' he said, 'not a God of priests and imams. I read the book,' (said with a blush) 'and I honour it, but the form of my faith is for me alone, and I alone will answer for it – to Him and to none other.'

We had a man come to see us who said Ludo should marry Crian, repent for all his debauchery and give his life to contemplation, alms-giving and the Haj.

'Don't you know there's a war on?' Ludo boomed, indignantly.

The man ignored this and criticised Crian for dressing immodestly. I thought Ludo was going to brain him.

'You dare to come in here and have immodest thoughts about this girl, to her face, and blame her for it?' he roared, looking like a dragon that had downed a tank of petrol. 'Get out! Scat you, you..!'

Such confrontations spread in story. It became

clear that Ludo was forming a conception of Islam that had been widespread already but never loudly espoused. Muslims who weren't offended by others' failings, but rather pitied them, who were glad to see a woman unhumbled – Muslims who had kept their eyes downcast in the presence of the severely orthodox – these people soon found a champion in Ludo, whose prodigious oral memory rapidly equipped him with enough verses and *hadiths* to best pretty well anyone in a quoting contest.

Very soon he had assembled a core of quotes and precedents, a body of knowledge he delighted to display. 'There shall be no compulsion in religion,' was one of his favourites, always followed with: 'That's the Holy Koran, by the way, look it up – book two, verse 256!'

'Religion is good advice,' was another we heard a lot, from a *hadith*, that one. 'Take care of your own selves. If you are righteous, the misguided will not succeed in trying to lead you astray...' was a riposte he made to any who brought a religious dispute to him, as many did. Those of us who feared a brutal application of Shariah Law were relieved to hear the familiar boom of 'God commands justice and fairness – Koran 16, verse 90!' along with my favourite clause in the whole book: 'One who is compelled without intending to violate or revolt is not to be blamed.'

This last was particularly useful in the prosecution of the war, though, as Ludo pointed out, Shariah's injunctions as to war were pretty well in line with our own code. It forbids maiming, injuring children, women and the elderly, as well as damaging animals, crops and buildings. The suicide sheep, swept-away towns and the odd enhanced interrogation we excused under the compulsion without intention clause, agreeing that we did not intend any of it, and wouldn't have done it, had we not been forced to fight off the unjust Invader.

There were two areas in which Ludo was radical. The first was the *hudud* – a table of punishments laid down by the Koran – which include amputation for theft, stoning for adultery and other dire consequences for alcohol consumption, fornication and bearing false witness.

'Do we not call him the All-Merciful?' was Ludo's line. 'These punishments are all very well in theory – I am sure we can all think of drunken thieves, liars and shaggers who deserved no less. But if these laws are God's laws, then these punishments are His also. Though these sinners may justly fear stoning and amputation in the next life – unless Allah is Merciful with them, as I expect He will be – they will not suffer them here on earth. Or at least not in Wales! Is not the sixth of the Six Pillars of Faith to believe in Allah's determination of affairs, whether good or bad? Well then, let us so believe.'

And no doubt some muttered that as a thief and a fornicator Ludo had much to gain by this interpretation, but some will always mutter. His other radical line concerned women. 'The Koran says God commands justice and fairness,' he repeated. 'So here it is: while I live women will have equal rights in all things. Anyone who seeks to oppress, limit, undermine or in any way restrict a woman merely because she is not a man will answer for it. And if I have got this wrong I will answer for it. But I will answer to God, and women's oppressors will answer to me, and I promise you, I am very far from All-Merciful. Got it?'

His high-hearted embrace of the Faith, and his love of philosophical and theological fun and games set a fine spiritual cement to the fashions inspired by Uzma. He was once challenged about the praying – five times a day, including once in the pre-dawn dark – wasn't it a bit much?

'Never!' cried Ludo. 'Haven't you tried it? It is excellent exercise, and a wonderful way to limber the body while humbling the mind. Give it a go. It's like doing yoga with God.'

His interpretation of Islam might not, perhaps, have been sufficient to convince his new spiritual brethren in far-off Waziristan or wherever that this was a man holy enough to die for under the guns of the Invaders, but it did – some said bastardise, others rejuvenate – certainly reinvigorate the religion and the country. And yes, it lead to trouble later, and a pretty strange turning in my life – but there I go again. It is not just my age that has me running out of sequence. It's all I have to remember, and the bits I'd rather not.

If we were going to clear the country of the Invaders it would not be enough to meddle in their computers. We had to rake them off the earth. We could not let their garrisons see one chink of hope between us. We had to bring everyone out from underground, arm and provision them and set them ready. If anything went wrong, if the Bug slipped, we would all be caught out of our holes and slaughtered. The Invaders' work would be done in a day and a night. And so we schemed and scrapped and as we closed in on our plan it became clear that Ludo might be about to get us all killed, and it was remarkable to me that he did not sink under the burden of the last word. But then it is a king's prerogative to hazard the lives of his people, and his duty to look confident while he does it. That is what makes him king.

Caravans! It was a stroke of I don't know what: I'm

slow to claim genius and wary of divine inspiration. But – caravans! Every year, every sunny day, the lanes and roads of Wales are jammed with them, have been since man first figured out the correct sequence of horse and cart. Well, next time you are stuck behind one, spare a thought for the revolutionary war. How do you move thousands of people around the country and God knows how many guns, without being spied from above? Crusaders, Road Kings, Excaliburs, Rangers, Quests, Free Rovers, Explorers, Venture VIIs: now you know why they call them such proud names! May Bank Holiday weekend that year was chaos on the roads. And of course the Invaders mounted road-blocks and spot-checks, but we had Theo chock full of sardine sandwiches, his buggy fingers flying over the keyboards, and if his hacked drones saw trouble the guns were thrown into ditches or over hedges, and everyone had a cover story – mostly 'going to see Grandma in Mold' – and most of the loads got through.

They caught one near St Clears, two girls and boy who sold their lives well, and another full of Semtex near Sennybridge. The boys there had orders to surrender rather than blow the load because we couldn't afford that road closed. They were hauled off to enhanced interrogation in Hereford. They could not tell more than they knew: drive the caravan to Cardigan and await instructions. The bangs were meant for the barracks at Aberporth but no one had told them that. Their names are on the Martyrs' Monument in Cardiff and their souls are in God's keeping.

The Invaders had read the same books I had on how you defeat an insurgency. There's one by a Frenchman, the Butcher of Algiers. Torture and summary execution, my friends, those are the time-tried methods. And they used them on us, and once or twice we had to use them on them. Traitors we shot: my department and my least favourite job. Some little terraced house in the back streets of Llandrindod, a rainy night, not a cat stirring and some poor turncoat tied to a chair in the kitchen and beaten bloody by the time I got there. We tried to be slow to convict, but once we moved we could not afford to be squeamish.

'Clip's coming,' they'd tell the poor sod, 'Cut-lip Clip is on the way. You know what happens then? Two minutes after Clip walks through that door you will be dead or singing. And sing well, or it'll be both...'

I never messed about. 'Why did you do it?' was my first line. That's the thing they wanted to say, even if they were terrified to spill another word. They threatened my family, they offered me money, they said they'd kill me, torture me, put out my eyes... They want to tell you this: they're desperate to share their reasons because part of them reckons that if you can only understand the whys you might begin to see other things from their point of view.

If they didn't answer that I'd give them the bullet. No hanging about. If they did answer I'd dig the rest out of them. Any hesitation and it was always the bullet. When they were dead we used to rag the corpse a little, before it was dumped, to spread rumours of vile torture, to discourage the others. You still wish you had been there, do you, you young braves? Sit in the pub sometimes, do you, listening to the old and their war stories, wishing you had had the luck to be born into the Generation of Heroes, the ones who fought for freedom? Thank your stars and count them. Go work out your heroism on the Playstation. If you weren't there you were bloody blessed.

Oh, I know what you want to know. When my time comes, when St Peter or Allah or whoever straps me in and addresses me with the pearly pincers I know what the question will be. Did you ever torture anyone? Did you ever make anyone scream – I mean really scream? Ever see someone go mad with pain? Ever looked into tormented eyes, wild with it, and promised a little bit more, unless an answer was forthcoming? Have you seen how a body convulses against the straps when the pliers prove stronger than the roots of fingernails? Can you see the disbelief in their eyes when they realise how far pain can go – that it has, in fact, no end? Have you heard the unholy sound a man makes when you wire his genitals? Or watched a girl screech and screech and beg as they beat her feet? Ever see your hands shaking as you tore up the cotton wool, to stuff in your ears, so you could block out the endless and broken way they always cry for their mothers, and carry on?

Did you ever smell a torture room, did you? The coppery blood, the piss and shit, the smell of agony, pain's breath, the rank sweet stink of it... Every scream has a smell. You don't forget the debris. The blood and excreta, the flayed-off flesh, burnt hair, the little bloody bits of someone glistening in the dirt – have you actually seen that? Or are you just content that it should all be done behind your back, for your sake, in your name? Did you ever say to yourself, over and over, I had to do it, we had to do it, it was war, it was them or us, it was an Enemy Combatant's life against the lives of who knows how many? They chose to do it, no one made them, they are worse than us, they would have done worse to us (if there was worse), they were on the wrong side and they chose it, they asked for it, there was no choice, they gave us no choice, they did it, they did it by their silence, by their guilt, they could have stopped it if they weren't so wrong – they were torturing themselves!

No, gentle God. The honest answer is I didn't torture anyone, ever, not with my hands. But I did have someone do it for me. A woman, as it happens, a proper little woman, neat as a pin and awfully handy with them. She was called Elsie and we were grateful for her. So give me the bullet, merciful Lord. I did that many times. It's the ultimate crime, isn't it, taking life? If it's worse than torture I don't know, but held to be, isn't it? Well I never made anyone else commit it for me. I shot plenty. I can't count them. So shoot me, dear good God.

We're coming to it now. Death or glory: not our preferred strategy, normally, but there comes a tide in the affairs of men when you either punch the buggers out or suck their toe-caps forever – as Shakespeare didn't exactly put it. Ludo had settled on his plan.

'Bring down everything. Bring the sky down on their heads, one strike, then in we go. We'll bomb the camps and castles open and give the garrisons the old All-For-One and ten minutes to choose...'

I still objected, as was expected: 'But what's to say they don't fight? They're bigger than us, even without the drones. We won't get them out of Conway or Beaumaris or even Cardiff bloody Castle without tanks, and not even the Irish can get us tanks.'

'The satellite missiles will help. They'll have no control, they'll be panic blind. Those conscripts have never seen us at fighting strength, and they know we honour a good surrender.'

'But they'll never buy it Ludo! They'll send heavy bombers, ballistic missiles, the whole basket. They won't care what they kill. And even if they do surrender you'll never get all the troops out – it took a year to get them in!'

'Tush, Clip. They won't have a clue until they're beaten, and we can't be stopped by bombers. We're too dispersed. Theo can hack them too, if necessary. They won't even *find* the country if he switches off their guidance software. We'll give the garrisons ten days to get themselves to one of the ports and we'll lay on ships – tankers. We've got them, haven't we? They can take the clothes they stand in and a bag of food.'

'And then what?'

'A few miles out and scuttle the ships,' Ludo said calmly, and winked.

'Get out of it!' I shouted.

'Oh, but you're cruel-cool, Clip! You were weighing it!'

(It was very funny at the time, which only made it worse, after.)

The planning went well, and the disposition of forces, thanks to the caravans, and we kept security very tight, and Theo said he was inside their system like a 'vood-vorm', and we were getting set to go, that early summer, when our enemies saw fit to make us the test-target for their second artificial army, and these weren't terracotta, but titanium and steel.

Automated Security Units, they announced,

would put an end to the insurgent threat. There were three types. A tracked, domed thing like a psychotic R2D2, mainly used for patrolling roads, though they could cross fields and climb shallow gradients, and two spidery things, one the size of an Alsatian, designed for urban warfare (it could run up stairs) and then there were the big spiders, which were the bastards. The size of a pony, they could scamper all over the countryside, go pretty well wherever you could, and much faster. The Invaders unloaded dozens of these things and waited to see how many of us they'd kill before we worked them out, if we ever did. They had heat sensors, motion sensors, audio sensors, infra-red, and they could be controlled directly or let off the leash on their own. Anyone in the wrong place would be challenged: a rasping, automated bark.

'Citizen! You are designated potentially hostile! Kneel down or be fired on! Obey in three seconds, two, one...'

And that was in guard mode. In combat mode they just opened up. They were terrible good shots and armoured like the devil. Even a direct hit with an RPG had to be a bit lucky just to put them off their stride. The old Milan and Javelin missiles were better but we did not have many of those. They earned their nickname: Killbots. Two of them working together could slaughter an entire squad in a couple of minutes – fifteen professional soldiers, methodically shot to bits.

You can see one of each type in the National Museum in Cardiff, together with a film of one of the big spiders attacking. It moves like it's a bit disjointed, but so quick. It comes scabbing across a field towards you, firing. They tended to conserve their ammo so that their guns wouldn't jam but every shot was aimed. In the film the spider walks into an IED – an IED beautifully sited, shielded from the spider's metal-detectors and set off by Roger le Gallois, incidentally – and you have the satisfaction of seeing it blown to bits. Cheers all round, though there's no counting the numbers they killed.

Rog and Moose were chased by one in the early days of the deployment. Their retelling became quite a comic turn (they got away by jumping in the Teifi, which was amusing in that Moose couldn't swim) but I debriefed them after it happened and there was no laughter then.

'The wheeze of its joints and the suck-suck-suck of its feet through the mud – Christ,' Roger said. 'You know your worst nightmare? Right...'

Our nightmare came a few days later. We were over near Pumsaint, meeting with two area commanders, finalising plans for the rising. A place called Troed-rhiwygelynen – meaning 'little holly tree at the foot of the steep slope', which is a fair description. A close valley, thick-treed, the lower half of which was all strewed wreckage from the blown dam. We were wrapping up when a scout burst in shouting there was a patrol on the way, two trucks.

'Coming fast,' she gasped. We scattered. Ludo, Crian and I went out the back and up through the wood with five fighters. There was a Land Rover waiting half a mile away over the top, but that patrol was on us quick, too quick.

Betrayed! I kept thinking, betrayed! We were barely halfway up the hill and they were fanning out below us, their bullets plucking and hissing. Bark and woodchips, zipping ricochets, scatters of mud, the ground unstitching around you and that crack over your head, the devil's whip, which says he only just missed you that time. The fighters we had with us were very good, all old British Army Gurkhas, and they snapped to the drill, a classic fighting retreat, two covering while the rest fell back, then all cover them, and so on, a kind of fleeing leap-frog with a lot of metal pouring down the hill at our tormentors.

I've met one or two, like Roger and Moose and Crian, who do seem to flower in a battle. I've heard them singing and roaring in the fight, seen how they turn retreat into attack, watched them flank their enemies and roll them up, out-thinking them, out-shooting them, breaking their bravery and killing them. But I have never felt or fought that way when the bullets are looking for me. First I feel small and weak, shrinking up in my skin. Then I feel too big, an easy target, and wish to God I was an earwig that could cower under a stone. The sights of your weapon shake with your hands. Your gun feels small, your own bullets too few, too slow; you seem to watch yourself and your own death coming for you, flying at you on hot wings through the trees. You can't aim. Sweat runs in your eyes even though you're freezing. You can hear your breath panting, gasping like a snorkel; your vision turns tight and strange. You can almost hear yourself groaning with the fright of it, you think in whimpers and shattered prayers and all you want to do is run, run, run!

Twenty of them must have been on us, near enough, but the odds were shortening. The gradient was with us and plunging fire is hard to hide from. Our fighters were beautiful, it was like watching a dance – aim, shoot, move to next cover, aim again, shoot, shoot, down, change mags, up, shoot – and all the time they were talking to each other, curt and clear, co-ordinating, and I saw soldiers below us going down, winged or killed, and there was that sobby-screaming. Crian was ever so calm, lying prone, eye to the scope, with Ludo spotting for her and carrying her rifle when they moved. Every time it cracked there was another of them gone to make his accounting. The Barrett is a heavy old gun for a slender girl but it tears off heads at the roots of the neck.

Their attack stalled and we burst across cleared ground near the top and were into the last tree-line and if we could just hold on, hold them off... I had heard Ludo on the hotline to his brother and I knew Theo's drones must be on the way to close the doors of hell behind us. None of them would survive pursuing us across the open hill, even if they wanted to, against Crian.

Then it came. Exactly as Roger had said, so quick, scuttling quick and big, bigger than anything in nature, a monstrous insect. Your blood really does go cold, something gasps in through your mouth, plunges to the sick pit of your stomach and all the way down to your bowels. It was the first one I had actually seen. I didn't know their surfaces were sticky-coated so that they gathered their own camouflage from woods and hedges. It was a thing from a child's nightmare, bits of stuff hanging off it, and charging us. And though it came out of the wood so fast, into the open, its spider-legs stabbing it over the ground, it was no faster than Crian and in the seconds it took me to squeal in fear she had hit it four times and one of its front legs was smashed and now it was crabbed and slower, but still coming, and she hit it again and again – and how were we to know? We didn't know that its cold brain assessed all threats in a digital blink and targeted the most direct.

It shot her through her foot, thrust out behind her as she lay at her gun, and the strike spun her sideways, and it shot a bright spray out of her thigh, then one through her hips, and still she struggled to bring the rifle back to bear and every one of us was firing at it now, up and firing, and there was a flicker of red giant flame with white at the heart of it and the blast wave knocked me down. Roaring, then the echo of the roar, then nothing until the bouncing thud and patter of falling metal and earth. At first, through the smoke, I thought she had killed it. But there was a crater there: the Bug had squashed the spider.

We went as fast as we could run across the hilltop with the Gurkhas covering us and Ludo carrying her broken in his arms, as he wept and begged her not to die. We reached the vehicle and he laid her down in the back, stripping off his shirt to cushion her. She could not move, not an arm, not a finger. Her life poured away in a red drain. It ran out of the door and dripped from the chassis. She never took her eyes from his face.

'Love, Ludo,' she said, 'I love you, I love you, my life – I loved you, always, with all my life...'

And he tried to stop her, he said save your breath, darling, save your strength, we'll get you home, you'll be safe, I love you so much, you saved me so many times and now I'll save you, I promise you darling, don't die, I love you too much. She seemed to smile then and she said: 'I am safe, my love. I love you and I am safe.'

We survived, thanks to her, her courage and terrible skill. And we wept as we drove away into the dark-gathering hills. And Ludo said nothing, made no sound, as the tears ran down his face. He said nothing that night, as we lay up in thick forestry, waiting for the scout who would lead us away at dawn. Not until the contact arrived in a logging truck, when the first streaks of our tomorrow barred the east did he turn to me, suddenly, with some new and dreadful stillness in his face.

'I'll kill them all for that,' he said.

'Yes,' I said, not understanding.

'No. I mean no prisoners,' he said. 'Never again.'

And so it was not just my nightmare that fell that day, by the little holly tree at the foot of the steep slope, and not just Ludo's either. Crian was right – she was safe. Until that day our fight had been a great and honourable thing, so I believed. But afterwards – well. All-For-One meant something different then.

I bear my share of it. I found out who made the call, a silly old man who lived by the bridge where the valley begins to narrow, who had seen us going through and had visions of wealth beyond fantasy, wealth pouring down to his children and their children, his name living in some infamy, like Christ or Judas: the man who stopped the war and brought peace to half the world. He got my gun in his mouth. I can see his crossed eyes squinting up the barrel now, mad with desperation for – what? For someone to wake him out of his nightmare, or for one more second of it? And then his brains are half over the back of his settee and half spilling down his parlour wall. It doesn't do to dwell, and no revolution can stomach traitors, and I came out of that house with my mind on Crian's dying eyes, not his – but still.

Still with me, are you? Want to hear the rest? I'm telling it for me now, as much as for you. And for the historians, of course. Historians – in the hope of your absolution! I'll not look for it, though as you see I think Ludo's is a special case. He never made a more tense call than the one to Theo to find out what he made of the Killbots.

'I need teenagers,' Theo announced, 'but grown-up kind, not idiot.'

'How many?'

'Maybe say thirty.'

'Got a job for them, then?'

'When I have thirty computers and thirty teenagers I have job, yes.'

'And you can sort these bloody Killbots then, can you?'

'Easy.'

'God is great.'

Recruiting thirty teenaged gamers without developmental disadvantages was easier than you might imagine. The war had grown everyone up. We put them under the control of a dreadlocked youth from the Rhondda known as Jimbo Looney, sent them north for training, then brought them south again to a newly appointed pothole near Ystradgynlais: dry, secure and, thanks to the computers, very warm. Jimbo and his cohort went a bit pallid in their weeks underground but they didn't seem to mind.

Towards the end of July it was still raining, Ludo hadn't smiled for a month, and we were ready. We set a date for R-Day (Revolution Day, Resistance Day,

Our Day, what you will) and determined that its first shot should serve as a diversion as well as a signal of intent. Their transportation programme had not been a great success but our enemies had not abandoned it; naturally, we had infiltrated volunteers into the emigrant population. Before dawn on R-Day they would blow up the Dylan Thomas Dome near Meknes, in that region of Morocco where those who had taken the ICU bribe had been resettled, along with those whose homes had been demolished for the dam-construction programme. And then Wales would rise, and England and Scotland too, we hoped. In the double dark of the back of that night, in a cave near Sennybridge, I stared into oblivion, reviewing the state of our islands, a state which, whatever happened, would vanish with the morrow.

There are fifty roads across the border, two bridges and the railway tunnel. Most of the crossings were closed and all were guarded by our foes, either manned or patrolled by Killbots. Eastwards, England was controlled by the Unity Administration and garrisoned by the enemy and their turncoat allies in the

British National Army – allies who could be relied on only to follow whoever would pay them. Further east still, across the channel, the World Unity Government had its claws sunk in the guts of Europe.

In a few hours the uprising would begin and either deliverance come from the west, as it had before, or the defying light would be snuffed. If we met success the fight would spread through the British Isles and perhaps beyond; three nations might rise and throw off the invader. If unsuccessful, a week would see our end. How would my death come? I had plans for a bullet from my own pistol. Beyond that, my only worries were for Ludo and Uzma. Our enemies would put them in cages. As the minutes trod on I resolved to see Ludo dead before he was captured, and prayed that Levello had similar provision for Uzma. Then again, she might be on a boat now, bound for some distant obscurity. He was a cunning man, Levello.

I was dropping off when a stir at the back of the cave told that Ludo was up. It must be time for the prayer before dawn; day was coming on. And I felt a sudden, breathless sense of the brink before us. Was this insanity? Had we, provincial as we were, put our own interests and those – as we saw them – of a small land of green rumples above and before the massed benefit of the peoples of the wide world? Too late to answer, now. I wished I could see Uzma again and talk to her. She knew more of the world than any of us. Through a half-dream in which I saw her, and sighed, a hand came, from a place which seemed distant, but was the darkness of the cavern.

'Clip, are you awake? It's started. They've blown the Dome.'

'Ludo...'

'Good morning,' he said, and I heard a smile in it, the first anyone had detected since she died. 'Happy Rebellion Day.'

Around the cave-mouth shapes moved, black against the paling stars. We piled into three vehicles and wended down, without lights, towards the barracks at Sennybridge.

The plan had us going in with the second wave – I had argued like a horse-haggler to stop Ludo leading the first. We would secure the base and establish an operations room from where we would direct, as well as we could, the actions of the battle. All over Wales, I knew, attack orders were being received – mostly read as texts to phones which had never been switched on before. We had arranged a distribution to hundreds of section commanders. I thought of hands shaking, mouths suddenly dry, of realisation, everywhere – this is it! And because they knew nothing of our Bug, nothing of our access to the drones and Killbots, most of those reading the orders would surmise they were a death sentence. One line of reassurance was all we had allowed, on grounds of security.

'Trust the fight will be fairer than it seems – the odds will favour the brave. Ludo.'

Far away in some steel-ringed bunker our enemy would be springing for his weapons. They would read some of the messages – perhaps all, we could not gainsay it. They would realise the go-code had been given and they would have a sense of the scale of the rising. All now depended on the Bug – could he blind and deafen, prevent the co-ordination of the defence? Would the programmes he had written for the drones, and such direct control as he would take, mesh with the timings of the attacks? We had made it as simple as we could. The assault on Sennybridge followed the same pattern as all the rest.

We were still two miles from the target when it started. Two huge explosions folded into one detonation, an eruption of light and noise and blast. Fountained bursts of fire and debris flung up, then a rumbling pause, then shots. Two of Theo's drones attacked a flight of helicopters which had been warming up for their dawn patrol. All were destroyed, along with the crew's mess, the armoury, the maintenance hangars and the canteen. At the same time, so it must have seemed to the defenders, their Killbots went berserk. Jimbo Looney himself was on the keyboard, so we learned later, and he turned a pack of four on their stewards, on the guards, on anything that moved inside the wire. Then he assaulted the lines where the soldiers were billeted and the first wave swept in behind.

There is an old story, probably a myth, that Saint David once distributed leeks to his fighters, ordering that they be pinned to the Welshmen's battle dress so that they might know friend from foe in a muddy struggle with the Saxons. The story says the stratagem was a great success and the Welsh that day gained victory. We copied the idea, with three finger-daubs of metallic paint (scratch-remedy I think it was, silver, for cars): one on the left shoulder, one on the chest and one between the shoulder blades. The idea was to prevent death by friendly fire – the drones and Killbots could see it clearly – but we were not convinced it would be successful. So we kept space between the Killbots and the fighters: Jimbo and his crew pressed home their attacks, all the way to the muzzles of the enemy guns, where, kamikaze fashion, they blew their robots up. After that it was up to us. At Sennybridge I saw it work.

Others have written their accounts. It was not down to Ludo – no. Even after Crian it might have been different, but the country was too small, the confrontation too desperate and desperately cramped, the stakes too high. We were as two Piranhas fighting in a coal hole: only one could live. In Sennybridge, and, we soon learned, around the country, the assault succeeded dreadfully.

Imagine being them. Suddenly the barbarians are over the wire. Your best weapons, your Killbots, turn on you and they are remorseless. Your own drones are slaughtering you. Your air cover has gone, your helicopters are carnaged, your computers won't talk to you, your phones are dead, anything in the air can't talk to the ground, your planes are blind, your artillery and fixed positions are being hit by drones or satellites, your mates are dead, your commanders are dead, no one's coming to help, you can't get a medic... Some will still fight then, the Specials will, some NCOs and sundry hard nuts, and some did – but the enlisted boys and girls? The ones who were just doing a job? In the back of many minds was the old All-For-One. If we just surrender we'll go home, they think.

We could not understand most of what they said,

the odd word here and there, but screams need no translation. By the time Ludo and I arrived – you should have seen him striding in, hot for it, looking for someone to fight! – our people were giving coups de grace to their wounded, and also to their unwounded. I saw a seventeen-year-old girl with a pistol striding along a line of prisoners. She gut-shot every one: three in the time it took me to get across and stop her. Guts is bad, too. Terrible.

'What in hell are you doing?' I scream at her.

'Killing fuckers!' she squeals.

I saw then how it would go, as I looked at her, with the bodies she had maimed floundering on the ground behind her. And I sensed that what we were doing we would pay for, though I had no idea how.

White flags flew but gave no succour. By the end of the day tens of hundreds of them were dead and the killing did not stop. The Roman general Agricola had thirty thousand men when he marched into our hills. Our Invader came with the same number, and two thirds as many corpses we burned or rolled, heavy and stiffening, into the never-surfeited sea. It was a terrible day, the Day of the Bug.

In the evening, when they had dropped every bomb and fired every missile, Theo sent his drones and satellites their self-destruction codes. Across the skies were explosions like higher fireworks. Everywhere people looked up and saw the tools of their oppression in flames and falling; the heavens rained dead drones. It was like watching the stars burn down. The other sight that lingers is Ludo, in a shot-up room in those barracks, when he realised that his once-dreamed dream of a merciful triumph was slaughtered, dying, screaming for clemency in tongues none cared to understand.

'What are they doing? Can't we stop them?' he roared, and when he saw that I could not, for that is what he meant, and that the curse he had cast the night of Crian's death was fulfilling, his face filled with disgust. Though it may not have been meant for me it fell on me, and something else went out for me then, and the time of my sorrows came on.

It took two weeks to leash the dogs of war. They were still killing prisoners on the quiet, in lambing sheds and out the back of pubs, until the day Ludo himself shot a man called Maldwin, because Maldwin had been caught charging people to watch prisoners fight his mastiff. That got the message out. And then the other people emerged, the good people, who had been hiding prisoners from the slaughter, concealing them in attics, woodsheds and spare rooms, and Ludo made his famous address – looking like hell – in which he thanked those people, granted freedom to all prisoners and said our darkest chapter was now closed, and all in the islands now were equal, and all life sacred.

Poor man, he looked like the very bandit our enemies had always said he was. The festival of horrors now over, we looked about us with cleared eyes. Like murderers the day after the maddening moon, blood rimmed under our nails, we stared at bitter victory.

We woke to a new country; an overgrown, ragged land, verdant and tumbledown, scarred and dangerous, mined and bombed, with spots like devil-sick where cadavers sank into the undergrowth. The Invaders had closed many roads rather than police them: they were cracked, pitted and overgrown. Bracken and heather had come down from the tops to meet briar and broome from the valleys. Woods had put out, hedges spread, ditches overflowed. There were flocks grazing the main roads and occupying parks in the city centres. Rugby grounds hosted teams of cattle. Wild dogs and crows as big as buzzards lived in evacuated villages where the populations had been transported. There were funerals everywhere at the end of that summer, when people realised their loved ones were not coming back from the struggle. I kept coming across them: crems and little graveyards in the rain, with clumps of small figures in black, desolate, with no coffin to follow.

Ludo went around with a face like a fortnight and barely spoke. In September he disappeared completely. The questions became frantic: where is he? I shook my head and counselled patience because it was not hard to work out. Sure enough, he reappeared with his nose sunburned, still not happy, but at least with a longer stride. He had been to Mecca.

All the while, the people, Ludo's people, looked to each other and to him and worried the one question none could answer: what becomes of a generation who have killed their way to victory? Oh, we did all the usual things. We rounded up the guns, rolled out post-traumatic-stress counselling, encouraged people to be open about things they had seen and done, and to admit what they regretted. Truth and reconciliation, Ludo decreed, were to be the orders of the day. But although the guns came in and the stories came out, there was a sense of things unfinished, abandoned not resolved.

The planet, at least, was in no doubt about the upshot. From the World Unity Government came the signal we had barely hoped to ever hear: the British Isles were to be an Autonomous Region. The occupying forces of England and Scotland, prisoners behind their own barricades since the Day of the Bug, trembling lest their turn should come, were withdrawn across the channel. Messages of congratulation came in from all over. And so the world and a slaughter-born kingdom waited to see what Ludo and Levello would do.

Part Two

I did not really understand how I lost the two people I loved. Ludo was off with his brother and Uzma in London. I was not invited. I suppose I sulked a bit. I tried to be philosophical. No one wants to know their dirty-worker after the deeds are done.

Ludo set himself up in a beautiful place in London, on the top of a tower in the river wall. He was always a dockside boy in his heart; he loved the water and the light and the great turmoil of faces. He loved being away, I suppose, from the scars of our victory. He loved London and London, now a free trading port, loved him back. Together they became rich. Ludo put a lot of money and effort into expanding her defences, building up her bulwarks against the sea. People started calling it Lundon, in tribute to him.

I didn't go there. There was a derelict old place on a hill I'd found. I did it up and settled, intending to surrender myself to contemplation, repentance and reading, and told myself I would write these memoirs, or something like them. But I never got round to it, because almost from the first day I had visitors, who soon all said the same thing.

'It's not that I want to speak out of turn...' they'd say, looking nervy, even though they would have already sought and gained assurances that no one else was listening.

'But it's Uzma...'

Had I heard what she'd said? Had I seen what she'd done? Did I know about the new mosques, and did I know how much they'd cost – did I know how many were planned? She'd lead prayers there, and made a speech here, and where would it all end, did I think? Frankly I had no idea, but that did not trouble my visitors, who told me anyway.

A Caliphate, a theocracy, that's where it was going. And what was Ludo doing about it? Was he on her side? Well, wasn't he? Didn't everyone know he was a Muslim now?

I was fed up of explaining that there were Muslims and Muslims, just like there were Christians and Christians, and Uzma was a good woman, and Ludo a good man, and no one need worry, and each to their bloody own, and just leave me be!

They wouldn't leave me be.

All the mutterings swelled to a scream a year after the end of the war, on a Friday at the end of Ramadan, when Uzma lead prayers for ten thousand up on Crystal Bluff. Some idiots, and I know who they were, set off smoke bombs in the crowd. The bombs didn't kill anyone but the stampede did – ninety eight people, and over two hundred hurt. Suddenly Ludo's kingdom was split and smoking, like an oak struck by lightning. Oh, he made his appeals, but he looked confused, I thought, and, for the first time, irrelevant. There were no personalities involved, somehow, except for Uzma's. It was about tides, about tribes. The Traditionalists, they called themselves – though they were a scramble of faiths and disbeliefs – versus the Believers.

The Trads had their big jamboree every May day. For two years in a row it ended in sectarian riots in dozens of towns. And what did they want? Or rather, who did they want at the head of this hurdy-gurdy wreck of a thing? Me! Bloody Cut-lip bloody Clip, and it did not matter how often I told them I would have nothing to do with it. It was still me they chanted for. How the rabblement love to hate you until they need to love you! And the old networks, my old networks were active again – let's have Rebellion Day Two, they said, but this time let's get it right. Let's bring down the brothers and kill their wretched woman (they had other names for her) and you won't have to take over, no, no, just help us get set up with decent government, secular government, put the Believers back in their box, no one else needs to get hurt and we'll all be happy.

It rose to such a pitch and frequency that I almost said, right, let's get it over with, then. But I never quite did say that, never got around to saying it or not saying it again, because one fine morning when I was almost happy because I had recently thrown away my phone and put chains around the gate on the track – not that they would greatly deter my stream of supplicants – around ten o'clock, when I was just making my second pot of tea, a helicopter landed in the meadow and the only man I ever really loved came striding up the track.

'Lovely morning, Clip! Put the kettle on, mun.'

'It's already brewing, Ludo.'

'Are we talking tea now, or something stronger?'

He looked as bouncy as a young ram, though he must have been in his mid forties then.

'Come in,' I said, weakly.

'Dare I?' he said, grinning, head back and hands on hips. 'I hear you've an infestation of rats.'

'I keep telling them...'

'You can't tell rats anything, can you? Better just splat them, isn't it? Well?'

'I've done splatting.'

'Oh, we've all done that,' he said. 'Got any milk, or do I have to wring it out of something?'

I took him out the back. Ludo put his hands

behind his head and sprawled on his seat, gazing out at the Beacons, at Pen-y-Fan, as it rode up into the springing blue.

I set the tea things down and poured and sipped and waited.

'Biscuit, Clip?' said Ludo, with a look I knew.

'No thank you, they're for you.'

'Go on. Have a biscuit.'

'No, really, I'm...'

'You might like a biscuit. Look, there's a chocolate one, have that.'

'Ludo...'

'It's hard, isn't it, when someone keeps offering. You're tempted to take it just to shut them up.'

'I don't want anything to do with it!'

'But that doesn't matter, because you do have to do with it. A lot of people will bloody die if this goes on and you *do* have to do with it.'

'I've told them no!'

I was a bit frantic then. Ludo looked at me with something like sympathy.

'Look,' he said. 'It's simple.' He put his hand in his

pocket and came out with a pistol. He cocked it, pulled back the slide to check the shell was where it should be and flicked the safety off. I took a breath and felt my eyes widen. He looked beautiful, almost as beautiful as the morning, and I thought, oh well. It makes sense actually.

'Stop it, Clip,' he said. 'I love you but I'm damned if I'll martyr you. Is that what you want?'

'No...!' I said, and my coward breath came out in a pant.

'Good. Here. Take it. TAKE IT!'

I held it miserably, pointing away at the remains of the daffs.

'Now, if I'm not going to shoot you, are you going to shoot me?'

'Of course not!'

'It might solve a lot of problems. Civil war, for a start.'

'I don't care. I gave you my life, Ludo...'

I stopped. We stared at each other. A buzzard called, high on the mountain.

Ludo shivered, suddenly.

'By Heaven,' he breathed. 'You even sounded like her, then.'

We drank our tea in silence. Ludo put down his empty cup.

'Right. I am sorry for your troubles, dear Clip. I know you didn't ask for them. I can see you have all you need here.'

'Almost,' I said.

'What do you lack?'

'Peace.'

'And a woman! Well!'

'I'm fine, really.'

'Wouldn't you like a woman?'

I looked at him curiously. 'What on earth makes you ask that, after all these years?'

'Well, despite what they say...'

'What do they say?'

'Oh, you know.'

'No, Ludo, I honestly don't. What do they say?'

'They say you're asexual! Or that you love me! Don't think I'm not flattered by the contrast!'

'So? Why do you come here talking to me about women?'

'Because despite what they say I know there is a woman for you.'

'Oh really.'

'Uh-Uh-Uzma!'

'Ludo, please.'

'Don't deny it! You love my brother's wife. You've been in love with her forever. I've seen you Clip. It's alright. I don't blame you.'

'What do you want?'

'I want you to come to a meeting.'

'Why didn't you just send for me?'

'Because this is going to be a meeting between the Believers and the Traditionalists, and Uzma is going to represent the Believers and you are going to represent the Trads and between you you are going to have it out and make friends and end this bloody business, and put my kingdom back together again, or I am going to lash the pair of you together and drown you like kittens in a barrel of grog. So I wanted to invite you personally, and hear your gracious acceptance. Unless you'd rather shoot yourself? Or me? Well? What's it to be?'

'You are crazy.'

'Crazy!' he roared. 'Crazy? Why didn't you say so thirty years ago and save us all the bother?'

We laughed wildly. When we had calmed down he looked at me with expectation.

'Where's the meeting?' I asked, suddenly tired at the thought of another battle, though I can't deny my heart was as high as heavy, at the thought of seeing her again.

'Oxford.'

'Why?'

'Why not? Good ground. In the middle – neutral.'

'Damn it! Neutral! What's neutral? I'm neutral – don't you see?'

'Clip, I do see. But what you must understand is, these people don't have anyone else who can stand up to Uzma, and they've chosen you. Don't you think I'd do it, if I could? But I can't, and Levello definitely can't, and it's Clip they want so – there.'

'What does Levello think of this insanity?'

And Ludo smiled his smile and I swear I could have hit him. Game over, again.

'Levello thinks it's a fine idea,' Ludo grinned. 'As a matter of fact, it's his.' (A pause.) 'Have we run out of tea?'

He drained another cup and said we were on our way. It was pointless to splutter. I stuffed a bag, locked the house and allowed myself to be introduced to his pilot, a young man called Reda. He was lounging by his shiny machine, a great glowing wasp in my first meadow.

'It is an honour to meet you,' Reda said, touching his heart. 'You are a legend to me.'

'What nonsense have you been giving out?' I glowered at Ludo. 'Well, Reda, if you can bring me home safe you will be a legend to me.'

Reda laughed, we all climbed in, the thing shook like a mad dog and then we were on our way.

'First time Clip?' Ludo said through the head-phones. 'We could have done with a couple of these in the war, well?'

'I'm happier shooting them down,' I managed, with some sort of grin, but it wasn't true. What a wonder is a helicopter! The mountains rush-rolling under you, and then up, up and the shine of waters rise to meet you and the knolls of the Cotswolds and the cathedrals on their islands – and all the boats! The big ships towed silver arrowheads and flew flags of smoke. The little ones snipped about and I thought God, I have been missing all this on my mountain. I felt rather sad. Then we were landing on the roof of a sort of boxed cathedral in Oxford, which Ludo said was a college.

'We're announcing the conference this evening,' he said, 'so it may be busier tomorrow, but you'll have a quiet night.'

It was Ludo-logic. The later you tell them, the fewer turn up, the smaller the riot. He showed me to my room and prepared to leave, saying there was much to do.

'There's some books there,' he said, pointing at a shelf. 'You'll be alright, won't you?'

'I'll be alright.'

'I – I miss you Clip. I read now...'

'I heard! I'm proud of you, Ludo.'

'But I miss you reading.'

'I miss it too.'

'Ah well! We'll do it again, won't we?'

'Will we?'

'No doubt,' he said.

After he had gone I sat on the bed. If I had been a drinker I would have had a few. Perhaps I should become a drinker, I thought, sniffing, and ran a bath. While it was filling I looked at the books. They all belonged to something called The Bodleian Library; they were not supposed to have been removed from it, and threatened severe penalties on whoever had. Free downloads of all texts were available, they said: originals were to be consulted only in the Reading Rooms. I knew the culprit, I realised. The books were all marked Mi – Fic and were by people called Mitchell. Ludo, I suspected, had gone into The Bodleian Library and helped himself to a chunk off a shelf at random. I took one down because the title pleased me and opened it somewhere near the back.

'My uncle would quote Luther: 'Whilst friends show us what we can do, it is our enemies who show us what we must.'

Hmm! I thought, who is this person with an interesting uncle? I took the book to the bath and turned to the first page. Several hours later, having extracted myself from a bath which had turned cold, I put on some warm things and burrowed under the thin covers. I was perfectly happy, hundreds of years and thousands of miles away. This Mitchell was a great man. I wished I could have read his book to Ludo, he would have loved it – trade, ships, intrigue, history, a strange culture and a beautiful woman: all his favourite things. Outside bells rung, songs of halves and quarters which suggested the hours were getting on with themselves.

It was gone midnight when there were heavy footsteps on the stair outside and a knock on the door. Partly annoyed at the disturbance and partly hoping it was Ludo, I jumped up. Something checked me – a thought of the mysterious uncle, friends, enemies, and old habits not quite dead, and I reached into my bag before crying, 'Come in!'

If I didn't like the look of my guest he would be flying downstairs with a spray of his brains preceding.

The old door winced open. When I saw who it was my hand came up empty. That was the second time I restrained the shooting of Levello, the Mountain King.

If Ludo was as big as a barrel then Levello was the mass of two. Darker than his brother, with a slower smile and deeper eyes, Levello had been changed by the war. No longer the roaring boy I remembered from the Bear hotel, nor the cunning war-leader, aglow with pride of his Bug. Nor yet Uzma's young husband, attentive and wry-smiling his love. No, Levello was different now. He seemed to tow more weight. He was carrying a package wrapped in tissue paper. He put it down on the table, straightened, and spread his arms.

'Clip,' he said, kind and warmly. 'Come here mun, give me a hug.'

It was like being mothered by a mammoth, and it's not often I had the chance to feel small.

He took me by the shoulders then and studied me.

'Did I disturb you?'

I liked the way the tense disguised the real question.

'Not at all! Well, I was in a book...'

'I'm sorry. Have you any tea?'

'Sorry?'

'Is there any tea in the room?'

'Yes! And a kettle. Sit down, Levello, do.'

The only chair squeaked at his weight. He set his elbows on his knees, his chin in cupped palms, and watched me fuss about.

'So something's wrong,' I said, carefully pouring the water.

'Yes,' he said.

'Can I help?'

'I fear so, Clip.'

'Tell me.'

'I dread it,' he said.

'Really, don't,' I said. 'I'm not afraid.'

He was sombre as a sexton. I laughed. 'Out with it, my Lord!'

'Clip,' he said, 'I am truly sorry it has come to this.'

'Heaven,' I said, thinking queasily of Uzma, 'what have I done?'

'Well that's it. You've never done anything – I mean, look at everything you've done! We owe you, don't demur it. My brother was ever a great man but with you at his back – a titan. And so for him, for me. Your brain, your heart, your honour, Clip – we owe them.'

'Rubbish! I'm just a fixer! Hundreds – thousands gave more than I did. Gave all, in fact.'

None of this seemed to cheer him up but I saw him see the moment.

'I've come to ask you a favour,' he said. 'The last.'

'Go on.'

'It's Uzma.'

'I thought it might be.'

And so Levello unrolled his dreadful tapestry. In the old, old days, he said, when two kings disputed, they would fight it out, or have two champions do it for them. I said I was aware of the practice. And would I agree, he persisted, that the split kingdom had chosen Uzma and me?

I conceded the point, gracelessly. 'But Ludo said we were to have it out and make friends?' I added.

Levello gave me a look.

'Friends of a kind,' he said.

'What kind?'

'She's never been a woman to take prisoners. She loves you Clip, but she knows what you're there for.'

'What am I there for?'

'To destroy her.'

'Destroy her? How destroy her? I'll never do that! I love her – I mean, I love her back. You love her! Of course we can't...'

'And she'll destroy you.'

'What is all this "destroy"? That's not the way, that's madness, war, you can't – I can't...'

'You know in the rugby...'

'What about the damn rugby? I hate rugby!'

'Rugby keeps peace by a pantomime of war. Think of it as rugby.'

Well, I almost went back to my bag, pulled the thing and shot him. How dare he talk to me about bloody rugby when the breath before was 'destroy my wife'?

'I'm not going to do it, whatever it is.'

'You must. You must stand up and tell the truth – and the truth is that these islands do not want religious government, have never wanted it since they cut off that king's head. And Uzma will flail you with the other truth, which is that maybe half the people do want to live for God, and that God is higher than all kings and princes, including Ludo and I, who have anyway sworn ourselves to Him. You will counter that not even Allah concerns Himself with something as small as running a country. Knowing all and seeing all is not the same as being responsible for all – He gave us free will that we might order our own affairs. A godly country we will always aim for, but a God-bothering one we shall not be, or something – you're the one with the words,

Clip! You can do this! You can do it beautifully.'

'Do what?' I shouted.

'You can get her to say it!'

'Get her to say what?'

He jumped up now and paced forward, towering over me like an elephant, and he poked his great snout down at me and said quietly, eagerly and with all seriousness, 'Get her to say she knows what God wants. That's against the book. Get her to say that and you've got her.'

'But – but – I've already said it haven't I? I've said God doesn't want...'

'No, you've said what God concerns Himself with, and what He leaves to us. That's all OK.'

Levello backed off. I felt dizzy and I heavy-sat on the bed, head in hands.

'Then what?'

'Oh, then she'll go on about God's law or whatever, it doesn't matter. You stick to your guns. Anyone who says they know the mind of God is in schism at the least, a blasphemer at the outside. And all those firebrand boys who have egged her on to it will be sick as pike, because that's how they go about, saying God thinks this and God thinks that – and it's all against the Holy Book, none of it comes from the Prophet, peace be upon him. It's about power for them and they bloody know it. Muhammad, peace be upon him, faithfully recited what the angel Gabriel told him, which is, live a good life, pay the alms levy, believe in God and the Last Day, fear God, and don't go around telling anyone you know better than God. It's in the Koran: you can look it up.'

'Well,' I said bitterly, 'if I'm going to do this I better had look it up, hadn't I?'

'I've got a copy here,' Levello said quickly, and plucked a beautiful green-bound book from his pocket.

The look he got off me then would have curdled custard.

'I'll just put it here,' he said, sheepish.

'That's it then, is it?'

'Well, you will have shot her fox.'

'And what? We shake hands and have a cup of tea?'

'Sort of.'

'Sort of. Meaning?'

'She's got to shoot yours, too.'

'Go on.'

'Oh, I imagine she'll say you are an infidel and an unbeliever, and possibly even an enemy of God, and that the fire is waiting for you – which is what it says, in certain circumstances, and she might go so far as to pronounce you one of those who God says should be killed by the Believers.'

'Great. Thanks.'

'It will all be fine.'

'I don't see how.'

'But you will!'

Levello made ready to go, with many reassurances and one in particular: 'Don't worry. When the moment comes Ludo will come between you. He will sort it. There'll be a judgement and then it's over.'

'What's the judgement?'

'Up to Ludo.'

'Do you know it?'

'I have an idea,' he said. 'But I'd rather not say.'

'Death?'

'No! No, nothing like that..! Oh, and there's one more thing – don't look like that, Clip! It's about your clothes.'

'What about them?'

'We think you should go smart but casual, you know, send a visual signal?'

'Oh, right, I've got something quite smart...'

'Yes, but the thing is we want you to wear this.'

He picked up the package and passed it over.

'What is it?'

'Have a look.'

I tore it open, too tired for delicacy. And there it was.

'Oh no. Never. No way. You're having me on.'

'It's perfect!' Levello laughed, clapping me on the shoulder with a paw that almost felled me. 'And it's your size. Tailored specially.'

It was a rugby shirt, the red rugby shirt of Wales. Number 10, of course.

'How can you even talk about destroying her?' I tried, one last time, as he left.

Levello was half through the doorway and so large he could barely turn in it, but he did, and looked at me with a stony glitter, eyes like a viper suddenly, and I thought oh yes, I remember you now, and your brother, and me.

'Because I really do love her,' he said. 'And because I want her back.'

She wore white, pure white, with a rune of gold in the hem. They had us not on a stage but in a pit formed by banks of spectators, facing each other across a sort of table. There were cameras and scrums of people, a crowd stretching that old room to the creak of its timbers, and there were guards with guns at the door. The cameras were the worst, like they didn't want to miss a pore of this scrap between the ugliest thing in the land and the most beautiful by far. And there I was in that bloody shirt, feeling like the surliest insult, like I'd done it deliberately, as if I wasn't foul to the eye already. I was sweating cold and dizzy as a drunk.

God bless her, she saw it all straight away. She

might have foreseen it months before by the way she caught my eye the moment we were brought in, and by the way she smiled at me with all kindness, and seemed to leave everyone else behind as she came over. She came towards me like grace.

'Clip,' she said, and held out her hands.

I took them both and sank to my knees.

'My queen,' I said, staring down at her perfect toes, two of which I could see.

There was pandemonium then! There's your visual signal, Levello, I thought. How's that? The straw dummy you've placed at the head of the Trads, kneeling to the true Queen of the Believers! All over, I thought, I give up.

Her supporters thought the same. They went wild. Even wilder went the Trads – howling at them, howling at us, howling at Ludo and Levello, howling like furious dragons.

'Get up Clip!' she said, pulling me to my feet. Keeping my hands tight in hers she turned to Ludo and Levello. She raised her chin, and then one eyebrow, and do you know – you can check it, thanks to those cameras, it must be somewhere – just that was enough! They fell silent. All of them fell dead silent.

'Here we are, my lords,' she said.

Her voice was – was – music. Soft and humoured, without a shake or a single fear: low music which carried to every corner of the country. I could hardly stand I was shaking so much. She kept a steady grip of me.

'Here we are, my lords,' she said. 'What would you have us say?'

I saw Ludo swallow and I thought here it comes, Ludo speaks now and it's over. Who can command like her? He could talk typhoons now and it won't save him or his brother. They're finished. But Uzma continued.

'Anything you bid us we will do. Right, Clip?'

'Speak, then!' Ludo cried, before I could answer. 'Speak for your factions, your beliefs, for the grievances and for all those who follow you. Restrain nothing of your hearts and conclude with how you will be satisfied.'

You would never have known that he had sown everything up, from curtain up to call.

'Who will begin?'

'Uzma!' I squeaked.

'Clip!' she said, in the same instant.

Anywhere else someone would have laughed. Ludo permitted himself a smile.

'Clip?'

'Uzma – the lady first.'

'As the lady, Clip,' Uzma smiled, 'please, I beg you, say what you have come to say.'

Oh Lord! I thought, as she turned her cool face to me, Oh help me! And perhaps He did. Uzma did, I know that: she squeezed my hands suddenly, a pulse of a squeeze, like she was handing the thing to me because she trusted I would not drop it, as if I could not drop it. So – I just opened my mouth.

'Uzma. I think they – I think we fear you. We fear your conviction. In our conception there are so few certain things. We love people, many or few. We love things, feelings. We are loyal to an idea of these peculiar islands and their particularities, as they have grown and changed and collected here in the thousands of years. Ours is not so much a country of convictions, Uzma. We have leanings, sympathies and tastes, even adorations. We have loathings. But if you could see all these things as colours, or currents, you would not see them arranged in ranks, in bright primaries, or flowing in one direction. If we are absolute for anything it is for the aberration, the less than absolute. The exception that proves the rule is something we cherish for both its sides. This archipelago of modest tones and sudden brightenings has known every darkness, Uzma. Our story is thick with bloody chapters. Religious war. Class war. Political civil war, and wars against invaders. Believers have burned believers at the stake here. We have made torn corpses of men, women and children too – here and abroad. We want no more of it. And when we look at your faith, Uzma, and the way it is followed, we fear. All I have seen of it is kindness and nobility – and beauty, true. But I know more than I have seen – we all do. We have seen Puritanism, here, and rejected it. We have seen the oppression of women and the enthronement of bigots. I spoke of loathing, and we loathe dogma. The most powerful religion in the old world came here, and touched and held people inspired, and for the basest reasons, perhaps, we made it make an exception for us. And still our exceptions and aberrations caused death and suffering – for hundreds of years. We want no more. Your vast rallies, your chanting thousands, the million minds made one, and most simple, in its prejudices: we entertain these things, but only when it comes to football – or rugby. But we cannot, we will not accept them in the realms of politics or religion – those potent and most mischievous powders we prefer unmixed. And perhaps your truth alarms us.

'Perhaps we envy you your certainties, doubting our own powers, our ability to share them. Perhaps those tastes and weaknesses of ours for the commercial, the worldly, the junky and sleazy – perhaps our lacks of faith and our avarices are deep and secret shames for us. Perhaps we are subject to great doubt and sad confusion about how we have lost our way, and perhaps your upright and outright rejection of our more corrupt addictions fills us with an odd and uncertain envy of you. We are certain, though, that it is no religion, nor any ranking, nor dogma nor doctrined path that will lead us on from here. Though we have fallen steadily out of love with religion, we are still people of faith. We demand the right to find our own diverse ways, according to our own strange hearts.'

There was no roar of approval from the Trads, then. I saw some heads shaking, some nodding. There were winces. Jaws were stroked; people shifted in their seats. There was a rumbling buzz, like bees. Perhaps they felt I had stated our position with too much sympathy, with insufficient rambunctiousness. Their heads now turned to Uzma. She surely knew I had left her two open paths, and that a single step down the wrong one would bring riot and open hell.

Uzma had no need to draw herself up. She always stood straight. Her bright gaze lay kindly on me, and there was a smile in it, though not in her tone as she answered.

'It was kindly spoken, Clip,' she said. 'I don't doubt your sincerity. You describe a tribe that some would say is lost and loitering in a wilderness. You can imagine how we feel, people of my faith, when we see you as you have described. The hordes who seem in love with oblivion, with alcohol and lust. The lives wasted in front of screens which preach so much materialism. So much trash! How many relationships, how many families are shattered by one too many? Who can count the vows forgotten or drowned in the beat of the clubs, by the fights and the fucks? How much havoc is sown by the flash of a pair of pins in a short skirt, by the swell of thrust breasts? I am not condemning!' she shouted, as an angered growl rose from the packed ranks, and another answered it from her supporters. 'Your own vocabulary is honest. Don't you call your nightclubs meat markets? Don't you call your women slappers, slags and sluts? Don't your young go out fighting and shagging and drugging because they lack the intense centre which holds us steady? Can you blame us that we turn our faces from these things? Does it offend you that we have another way with our liberty than getting hammered on Brains and cider? Don't you agree, secretly, that it is better, kinder and healthier in all ways to abstain? I don't expect you to admit it. Maybe I am wrong. I am just trying to show you how we see it – how our religion sees it. And don't you think we don't want to share the good news with you? Don't you think we would rejoice if you turned your faces from that emptiness towards the fullness we experience? And don't you know that our religion obliges us to share this perspective with you? To hold it up and say – look. There is light and calm this way.'

They rumbled and they roared, both sides now, and young braves in each camp gestured derision and challenge to each other.

'Hold before you damn me!' she shouted, and there was a flash of her, the warrior queen she had never allowed herself to be – had never been allowed to be, in her place as Levello's wife.

'I have not finished. Clip speaks of faith without religion. Clip speaks of freedom to demur, to swim against the tide, to make exception. Clip speaks of history. Of your land. Of your peculiar traditions. Clip speaks of something, some lodestar, some hazy God or science, which you follow in your own ways. And the question Ludo asks us to answer is – how do we live together? Can we not devise a system of respects? For example, we Muslims can abstain from mass rallies, if you – non-Muslims – can refrain from confronting us with so much that offends us. Refrain from judging, from criticising, from feeling threatened, most of all. Can't both sides be quiet in our convictions? I am not willing to hide my faith, but I am not ashamed to practise it modestly. Can't we join in contemplation and experience? What's all that matters, in the end? Love above hate, above all. Listen! I have proof. I love my husband, I love my God, I love this earth, this land, its ruler, Ludo, and I love Clip – it's true! Don't ask me, any of you, to turn from any of them. I can only live if I can love all these things. I won't fight any of them. I won't fight but for them. And for them I will fight to my last breath.'

And with that she took my hands.

'We will not fight,' I heard my voice say, my croak, so spitty and mangled.

'Anything, but we will not fight, ever.'

We embraced.

'I love you,' I whispered, as a rush of wonder went through the crowd, a rush of confusion, cowed, something like jealousy or fear.

'And I love you, darling Clip,' she said softly, her lips against my ear. We squeezed tight. Perhaps our speeches had intoxicated us. It was as if we had both been taken somewhere where no one else was. And – Lord forgive me! – all I wanted then was her, I wanted her, and she knew it and did not draw away. Only she leaned her head back and gazed into my eyes.

She smiled. She nodded. I turned to the kings, still holding her, and saw, in that instant, how the trick had worked. And I was a fool, a holy fool, because the looks on their two faces were so knowing, and their eyes triumphant, though they kept their expressions still – while her face was merely beautiful, alight with some simple thing.

Ludo stood up. We drew apart, still holding hands.

'That is good,' he said. 'And almost good enough. You know what you have done, and here undone. You have brought this country into the very mouth of destruction. It was gravely wrong. Innocents have died for your vanity, for your rabbling and your lust for power. All that must end. We cannot allow you to return to your strongholds. Nothing can be as it was. Some may say you deserve punishment, but you are not to be punished. You are banished, banished from each other and from the madness you inspired. Uzma. Will you go with your husband?'

She was still looking at me, at me! And still she held my hands.

'I will,' she said, without the tiniest hesitation.

'Clip, you will go with me.'

'Yes,' I said, and I never took my eyes from her while they led us apart, not until they took us out through different doors.

It took people a while to work it out, and I was one of them. Levello's summer house in the skirts of

Snowdon had been massively enlarged, a low castle complex now filled half that high away valley. There they buried Uzma, in comfort, in freedom, with anyone she chose to see, free to come and go, but buried there, still. She still made speeches, and still supported causes and endowed foundations and sponsored mosques, but even if she had wanted to shake it again, well, her staff had been broken that day in Oxford, when the world saw the way she held my hands, and took me to her.

Ludo took no risks with me, either. Reda flew us straight over the mountain where I lived and kept going, west and further west. We passed over my first home. There was Pembroke – there was Castle Terrace!

'Where are you taking me? Ireland?'

'Not quite,' said Ludo. 'Very like it, though, and it's right for you, Clip, I hope you'll love it,' he said, and grabbed my hand and shook it in an awkward way.

Reda did a fine job with the wind and the cliffs, holding the machine just over the tips of the turf, just long enough for me to jump out and for Ludo to shout, 'It's all there for you, Clip!'

He gave me a salute, which was strange, the only time I ever saw him do that, then Reda had the thing up and over, diving down to hammer away again, low across the water, back towards the land. I was left shivering like a stray, abandoned to my first twilight on the island. It was cold and wild. Under all that sky, behind a cloud of screaming birds there was a hunched-up little house, and so I stumbled in.

Oh, they worked it beautifully. They worked us like fighting beasts, lathered all ashiver, dragged into the pit, turned loose – and then! Let us and the whole world see we loved each other, that we would sooner die than harm each other, that everything else was nothing at all. Nations could sink, mosques and churches burn, people hang, castles and kings collapse and we would not blink if we could only see each other and hold one another's hands. Drunk in love like two silly pigeons, and caught and thrown away.

I lay in a cold bed thinking these things. It's all

there for you, he had said. A file on the kitchen table gave instructions about how the catchment tank worked and so on, and said that the boat would come monthly with stores. It would take orders for whatever I wanted. It was indeed all there for me, but that is not what he meant. He meant that the memories, the thoughts and the longing were all there, in the wind and every bird's cry, and that they were all mine for as long I lived. I writhed in shame, in wanting and in love.

Part Three

Gulls' eggs: I thought I would grow flipping wings. April was stormy; one blew for three days. You couldn't stand up in the wind. No boat came and I thought that was why, but then there was no boat in May either, for no reason I could fathom. I had only rice and what fish I could catch. Depending on a rod and line for your supper is not sport so much as anxiety.

In June it came. They would not even come ashore. They could have tied up at the little dock but they stood off, loaded a small boat and had a boy row it to and fro.

'Anything else you want?'

He was only young. His captain peeked from the wheelhouse, like I was some sort of gorgon.

'It's all on the list! A radio, for God's sake, I must

have a radio. That's the most important thing. Please try to get all the books and the tools, and the seeds. Pepper too, I need pepper.'

'OK.'

'And news – what's the news?'

'Wha'?'

'The Trads, the Believers – Uzma?'

'Don't know. Don't go in for it, like.'

'But there's peace?'

He looked blank.

'No fighting, no riots?'

'Don't think so... I haven't heard.'

'Thank God. And Uzma?'

'Don't know. Haven't really heard.'

'Ludo?'

'In London... isn't he? Saw him on the telly. Yeah. London.'

'What was he doing?'

'Can't remember. You know, talking. Like he does.'

'OY!' the captain shouted.

'What's your name?' I cried, as the boy pulled on his oars.

'Stephen.'

'Thank you, Stephen!'

'Alright.'

'I'm Clip. My name's Clip.'

The boy looked as though he might say something but he was almost at the boat. He might have smiled but then he was turning to catch the gunwale and the captain was on at him and that was that. I was back to watching ships, little slow bars crossing the horizon. My only human company was the crab potter who came some mornings, maybe twice every ten: once to sow his traps, and once to haul them in. He gave me one wave each time.

They came again in August. Every two months, I swore, as I ran down the path – every two bloody months!

'Hello Stephen!'

'Alright there.'

'God it's good to see you! How are you? You look well! Did you get the radio?'

'No radio allowed, Clip.'

I cried like a little kid. It wasn't the radio, it was the 'allowed', the thought that someone – that Ludo had done that to me, like that. Ludo... And because Stephen said my name. Just about pulled myself together by the time he came back with the second load.

'Who says what's allowed, Stephen? Who do you deal with? I like that pin in your nose! That's the fashion is it? Where do you live? Have you got some-one special?'

'I'm not allowed to talk to you,' he said, not with any relish.

'Oh but these boxes are wonderfully heavy! Tell you what, I'm going to have a feast tonight. Do you fish?'

'A bit, yeah.'

'What's your favourite?'

'Mackerel.'

If he kept his back to the boat and the captain – and the captain's friend, I noticed, along to gawp – and as long as I kept it very quiet...

'Stephen, you've got to get a message to Ludo.

Please, tell him I need to see him, it's vital, I've got to see him, tell him, there's something he needs to know.'

'No messages,' he said, shortly, flushing.

'No! Sorry, sorry – right. No messages. Sorry Stephen, it just came out. Mackerel! I love them too. Lovely, delicious fish, and so many! How's the world then? What's the news?'

He shook his head and pulled away.

'Is there another load?'

'One more.'

He came back.

'Have you heard of Uzma, Stephen, have you heard anything?'

'Only the baby thing.'

'What thing!'

'They say she's pregnant. They're on about it.'

I burst into tears again, then.

'I'm so sorry Stephen, to embarrass you. Will you tell them I am happy? So happy for her, so happy... send her my love, will you? All my love. Good lord, what a day! Quite a day for you too, all this crying, I am sorry. It's so – strange, isn't it? How are you Stephen, how's life with you?'

'Well, bit tight like.'

'What do you mean, tight? Captain not paying you properly?'

'No, well, it's the money thing, isn't it?'

'What money thing?'

'The thing with the banks. You know, the crash or whatever.'

'Go on.'

'Oh I don't know. The economy. All the money's been spent or something. Everyone losing their jobs. You're well out of it. With all this...' He waved a hand at the boxes, which now made quite a pile. 'Tidy.'

'You're welcome to it! Here, I'll have the boat. I'd give you a key but there isn't one – be my guest!'

We both forced a laugh and he settled back in the boat, preparing to go.

'That's the first time I've laughed,' I said, thinking don't cry again, he'll know you're mad.

'Will you come again soon?'

'Oh, I 'spect so.'

'Are they going to keep me here for the winter? How will you get to me? What's going to happen?'

'Don't worry,' he said, as he backed one oar, turning the nose away, 'we'll keep coming.'

'Stephen,' I said, suddenly, 'if it gets bad and you need something, money – I know where...' and now I hissed it, '*I know where there's gold! From the war!*'

We held a gaze until he reached the boat. As the boat nudged it, just before he turned away, I saw him nod. He knew I saw.

So much to think about! When I had hauled everything up to the house I made a meal of chops. After, the light lasting, I went for a walk to discuss things with the birds. I dreaded the birds a bit, at the beginning. There were so many and they didn't like me, until we got used to each other.

I greeted the Black Snappers: huge gulls which looked at you like breakfast. I thought of Uzma as I watched the Snake-Necks at their fishy business, and the Keep-Awakes all screeched like babies. The Bull Gliders recalled Ludo, and the Sea Parrots his people in their thousands. I met one of the three families of Chat Crows on my round. They know all about boom and bust, for all that their currency is ants. Out to sea there were Plungers, stuffing themselves on the big fish; they never went short. I bid them all good-night and barred the door. I checked my pistol for the hundred thousandth, time.

When the dark came it brought Boblins, crazed creatures. If you could whirl a drunk ghost around your head you might hear the noise of the Boblin. A pair nested under the house and she laid one egg, which turned into a smudge with eyes called Ludo-the-Littler.

I put the pistol away, guilty that I should ever have played with it as I did sometimes. As well as the birds there were seals, my mermen and maids. No one would find a mess of me, shrunk black beyond decay: come the day when I could no longer face another I vowed to go swimming with them.

Several times that winter I took up the gun to scratch no itch at my temple, to suck the muzzle, to taste its metal tongue. Again I put it by. I grew a love of storms. I summoned them, taunted them on. Once or twice the house seemed about to go. Elated, terrified, I prepared to go with it in the only way you can – yelling mad. The quiet days, icy still, when to look at the sea was to freeze, I spent in reverie. The house was well insulated but I could run the diesel less than half an hour a day. Cooking gas I husbanded as if it were the last on earth.

The lights of the refinery at Milford mocked my amass of darkness, until one heavy dusk. It was around the end of February, I guessed – I had lost count. I glanced that way and saw that the lights were doused. How long? Less than twenty-four hours, I was sure. Was it a power cut? War? I rushed out to the cliff and peered the other way, towards St David's and Solva. No lights there either! Only ships at anchor showed, their superstructures twinkling. Not war, then. In two hours of watching I made out the flash of a single car on the hill above Newgale.

It took me a long time to sleep and then it was only to wake again, to wake the way we used to in the war – suddenly up and pounding, as if you'd heard death step on a twig. The wind was coming from the land and I strained for what I thought it had told my sleep. Yes! And again! Small arms: two or three volleys and now nothing. War, then? Nothing persisted. Eventually I went back to my pile of coverings and burrowed in.

In the morning what could be seen of the world resembled itself. The crab potter waved, though he ignored my hails and attempts to gesture him closer. I pounded around in a wild frustration until I saw the lights of the refinery were back on, and one or two of the chimneys smoking.

The day after that there was a first warmth on the breeze and new birds around the island, little things blown in like confetti. I was up with the first of the sun, casting spinners. On my way home with two mackerel (neither much of a meal in itself) and coming down the High Road, a turfy track from the haunted ruin in the middle of the island, I caught it, chipper-chappering. It was too quick, scarlet, coming straight. I ran. As I made the house the monster was hovering a couple of feet above the parrot holes. The noise alone made me want to shoot it. I slammed in, dropped the fish and went for the pistol. The monster was closer. They meant to take the roof off, by the racket.

By God, I thought, there's nine cartridges. Just a little closer, I prayed, peering over the sill in the living room. I'll give the pilot two and the doorman two and save the rest for contingencies. I hope it doesn't misfire. I hope it's not Reda too, but whoever it is has made their choice.

'Clip!' boomed the voice through speakers, even louder than the hellish engine. 'It's me! Clip?'

I'll kill you, I whispered. (I had not noticed when I had started talking to myself but it was a long old conversation now.)

'Alright? Don't shoot the chopper, we'll need it!'

I'll kill you Ludo, I giggled, ecstatic, ducking down. Just you bloody wait.

More noise, a crescendo to drown my curses, before it pulled away. Now nothing, in its diminution, save every bird on the island screaming. That made me even madder. I stood behind the door, listening. Surely he would not be so stupid... Five minutes I waited, then ten and there was nothing but the birds.

Some I-don't-know-what, a beat in the air, decided me it was time, and I threw the door, took a step out, gun up, and he hit me, seemed to fall across me like a red bear. The gun was gone and I was tossed across the grass like a ball.

'And a happy St David's Day to you too!'

He had changed, I saw with shock, aged ten years in one. He'd got fat – all puffy, pallid. Soft. I up and threw myself at him.

'Bastard, bastard!'

He didn't move until the moment when he seemed to disappear. There was a blow to my kidneys as I fell past him, about a third of what it could have been, but it hurt.

'Clip! Stop it now.'

'You docky bloody thug, you murdering piranha, you shit you...'

'What do you want me to say? It was this or the firing squad – you know it.'

'You killed me anyway! You've killed me! I'm dead.'

'You don't look dead to me,' he said, and smiled down at me with an affection that made me want to cry. I turned my back on him, kneeling there, and cried all the more because it was stupid to be so mortally embarrassed by my filthy clothes and my hair, which in the absence of mirrors was the only part of my head I could see, and which had grown very long, and not neat.

'You look wonderful,' he said. 'You look great! What an advert for sea air. I've never seen you better.'

'You look bloody terrible. Call your dog back and go away. You wouldn't even let me have a bloody radio! You hateful, spiteful, lying – *traitor*.'

'Enough!' he shouted, and I heard him stamp up behind me. 'This is a disgraceful way to treat a guest and friend. Particularly one with so much news! Get up now Clip and let's have a cup, for goodness' sake.'

'You're no friend,' I said. But he had me – news!

God, news... I'll make him tea and get the story and when he's comfortable I'll put the flensing knife between his shoulders. The Black Snappers can have him.

Ludo looked at me strangely. 'Right you are,' he said. 'If that's the way you feel when you've heard me out I might even let you do it.'

'Well – Hell!' I shouted.

I ground my teeth while I made the tea, to make sure nothing else escaped. I banged it down in front of him.

'Thank you. You've made it lovely in here, Clip! I like the sculptures.'

'Found objects. Not sculptures.'

'But doesn't it take a sculptor to find them?'

'Don't soft-soap. I've had no soap for – eleven months.'

'Well. You smell clean. Like the sea.'

'You smell of lies and oil.'

He smiled quizzically. 'Perhaps it's a fair point.'

'Don't start telling me how lucky I am or I will kill you. What do you want?'

'Do you mind if we walk, Clip? I'd love to see around.'

'If you wanted bloody milk you should have brought some.'

He smiled.

'People have changed, Clip,' he said. 'They walk with their heads down, counting. Not the blessings either, not the world. You could bring them here and they would see it, I suppose, but – they don't seem to go about anymore. Can't afford to, at lot, of course. They don't look but in calculation. Their eyes are all turned in. It's all gone to getting and spending. Getting, the millions who can't, much. And spending millions, the few who can.'

'Boo-hoo. Has Uzma...?'

'Of course... you know. Stephen, was it? Yes, she has! A girl.'

'A girl! A...! I send – my love. Tell her – it's wonderful. Tell her I... Just – tell her.'

'You could tell her yourself.'

'You won't get me like that again. Never.'

'You know how it went after the war,' he said, as if I had not spoken, 'and how bright everything seemed.' (Had it hell.) 'And then when they took to competing faiths, some absolute for nothing, and the rest for nothing but the absolute, we settled that...'

'By killing me.'

'And Uzma, yes, and it hurt me, but you understood.'

'Not really.'

'Yes you did. And allowed it.'

'Given no option.'

'Indeed. And that should have been all. But then there was this crisis... did Stephen tell you?'

'No, and I don't care!'

'A bank went bust, one rotten bank, we thought. You know how careful we were in the war. Where it came from, who was keeping track, how much we were spending, on what, how we could get it cheaper – I mean – we've been good at it since the beginning! Had to be. And everything was set so fair, after, with the trade, with the ports, with London especially, we were making bullocking billions. Everyone was riching it.'

'*You* were.'

'I was! So then this bank goes. Monday it's shining, Tuesday dust – and a mob outside. They break in, find nothing worth taking, no one there. It didn't even have a vault. That was scary – a bank without a vault! Anyroad, it was all gone. The ones with their names on the papers are off east and all the rest are still living it up in London. Another bank goes the same way, and another, until people start to say – well. They start to say it's orchestrated. To kick out the ladder between top and bottom, to bust the rungs. To absolve the poor rich of the burden of the poor poor – that's what they started saying.'

'Atlas shrugged,' I muttered.

'Atlas gave the country a good bloody shake until anyone without a few million in Switzerland and a few million more in dry property fell clean off it, more like!'

'Could it have been orchestrated?'

'Officially,' – he looked angry – 'it was just a crash

in the markets, a crisis of confidence in the currency. Everyone wanted ICU and the old pound was paper.'

'What's the rate?'

'Five to one. On the black market, twenty-five.'

'How's the Treasury?'

'Well, that's it. It was piled with gold and ICU.'

'And now?'

'Gone.'

'Gone where?'

'Nobody knows.'

'Someone does. What does Levello say?'

'He says it's been spent. Atlas – right! The bankers, the traders, the speculators, the bonus boys and get-away girls, the water barons and the big merchants have had it, he says. He says if we want to get it back we'll have to wrestle a giant.'

'What's the giant?'

'That's the question.'

'Why didn't you let me have a radio?' I asked, as we walked back.

'It would have driven you crackers!' (He caught himself, then hurried on, colouring.) 'If you hadn't been so good at pumping young Stephen you would have been happier – admit it. I would have had your stuff dropped off by chopper except we thought you might shoot it down.'

'Where is my gun?'

'Here.'

'What's for tea?'

'Mackerel and bloody rice.'

'Oh – my favourite!'

'Get the rod then. I've only got two little spratty ones.'

'Fishing! Fan-bloody-tastic! I haven't been fishing for...'

'Do shut up, Ludo.'

'Decades and decades!'

'What's the blackout?'

'Power-sharing. Because of the electricity prices? First off we published the schedules so people could prepare for it, but then the flimmin' bandits – it all got out of hand... They did a right job on some of those towns. Nottingham, Cheltenham... it was like the good old days, Clip! Only I'm the bugger pulling down the curfews, now.'

'What flimmin' bandits?'

'Oh, well. You know. All sorts. Villains and thugs and people who've lost their homes and such, and a lot of kids since the school thing, and the universities... I hate to bang them up but you can't shoot them, can you? Of course when they fire at the police it's... well, you can see why people are buying Guardbots. And we had to bring back hanging. For piracy. There's no way round that. If the water can't go out and the oil can't come in – curtains.'

'Sounds like it's got past curtains. Sounds like an absolute disgrace.'

'I've got a bite Clip! I've got a bite!'

'Sorry, fishy.'

He battered its head on the rock, frowning. When it had stilled he smiled and held it up.

'But they're the most beautiful things, though! Look at that. Sea silver. Gorgeous!' Then, with an anxious look: 'Have you any butter?'

'Do you see a cow?'

'Only you!'

'Yeah? Know what I see, do you? A king reduced to a bloody boy. I look for Ludo – I see the mockery of the man. I listen to you, I hear a shrugging, simpering, kid-killing incompetent. A poltroon. A roll-mop. That fucking mackerel would have done a better job. Don't think of what we did. My bloody life... Don't mind a few thousand bodies, a stinking sea of bodies from here to Ireland. All in all – what's to mind? We did what we did. And for what? For shit in a fine shirt. For a stuffed-up dissipation. For the Peace Father! The Prince of the West – another good one. Another twat in a tall house with turrets, and a chopper. Lovely job, Ludo. A proper bank job. Make sure you never mind it. Take your fish and fuck away off.'

'You're right to be angry,' said the top of his head.

He was looking down at a sea-parrot hole. There were silver threads in his red. 'But I think I've had enough of the cold bath, now. Can you stop the histrionics, or have I come to the wrong island?'

'Got someone on Skokholm too?'

'Maybe!' he grinned. 'Maybe I have. Now, are you up for it? Or couldn't you handle your year in heaven? Lost your famous grip? I didn't think to find you so fragile. And skim off the curds, will you. It was kind, giving you all this, and clever too. So. Are you too far gone, or what?'

'You're madder than I am.'

'Show me one ruler who wasn't!'

'Oh, Lord. Whatever. Is there... some sort of a plan?'

'You know my brother. There's always a plan.'

'Go on then.'

'How about you cook while I talk? We need our strength. And if that sun's not just going down for a drink it must be time to pray. Join me?'

'No, thank you.'

'Right you are.'

'Fantastic.' He pushed his plate away.'I wouldn't have sold that for gold.' He looked at me. I looked away. 'Not for a cache of gold *from the war*!'

'He didn't leave anything out, I take it.'

'Not much! He's my nephew. Caswallawn's boy.'

'Ah. I liked him.'

'And he you. So. How's your relationship with God these days?'

I thought about it, washing up. 'I don't – do it – formally, but I pray a lot, sometimes. Now and then.'

'Living here... Must be like living with God, isn't it?'

'Very like. Wild as wind, busy as death, calm as the sound, and all at once.'

'And the other world, between us and Him?'

'The fairies and so on?'

'Ireland's not far, is it?'

'We could tune into the Dublin news – if only we had a radio.'

'So they are about then?'

'The spirits? I should say. The island's heaving with them.'

'Do you think they like you?'

'Tolerate. Sometimes I think they laugh.'

'Any bad ones?'

'I don't know if they go like that. I try not to disturb them.'

There was a loud tin clatter – just plates settling by the sink, but Ludo kept steady eyes on mine and smiled faintly.

'Have you heard the legend?'

'What legend?'

'About the island.'

'How I am supposed...?'

'Ah well, no. So. They say that there was an island, far to the west of the world, where no man would land. Nothing lived there but the souls of drowned sailors – God in Heaven! What was that?'

'A Night Boblin! They're back! Oh – maybe it's... He's back. How wonderful.'

'Back from where? Hell?'

'They go off when the winter comes. There was a nest under the house.'

'I see. Well anyway, nothing lived on this island but

the souls of sailors and a giant, a mad giant, because he lived there with all these soul-ghosts. If any boats came near he'd throw rocks at them. There's one sticking out of the sea...'

'I know it.'

'Yes, so, the thing about this giant was, he knew the secret of souls.'

'The secret of souls?'

'Yes. Because he spent so much time with so many, you see, and because sailors are great travellers, people of the world, their souls revealed many secrets, and the giant had a great deal of time to spend with them, and so he learned a great many things.'

'I see.'

'I'm sure you do. And that is why the giant was so angry and mad, and wanted to be left alone – because of what he knew. And it was even said that the giant knew other secrets besides the secret of souls.'

'Such as?'

'Such as, my dear Clip, the secrets of nations.'

A slam outside made him start then, but it was only the door to the generator shed. He must have unhooked it while he was poking around earlier, looking for somewhere to ambush me.

'I'll just shut that.'

I went out. A wind had come up from somewhere. Normally in the early dark it blows off the land, but tonight it seemed not to know where it came from or where it wanted to go. It wuthered about impatiently, moaning. I scolded it. I told it to go and lie down. It was warm; a sweet close warmth like spring. The moon wore a veil which made her look further away and older than she ought. I strained my ears for more Boblins but heard only the muttering sea.

'The secrets of nations,' I prompted him. He had been staring at nothing.

'Yes!' he cried. 'The secrets of nations. What are they, after all? Only collections of souls and ghosts. That's why the giant throws rocks at anyone who comes near. That's why he lives far to the west, as far from the land as he can. Because he has seen into the souls of nations and he wants nothing whatever to do with them, or anyone from them, either.'

'Can't say I blame him.'

'No, you can't blame him at all.'

'But?'

'What's that, Clip?'

'There's always a "but" with you, Ludo. And legends have them too, or an "and".'

'That is true. And so, or should I say, but – the story goes – or at any rate so it used to – but – if you could find a way to the island without the giant seeing you coming, if he was asleep, say, or distracted, and if you could land without him smashing you with gigantic rocks, and if you were able to face him, which would be hard, because of all the ghosts and souls casting dreams on you and making you fall asleep, then, the legend says, if you could only face him and fight him...'

'Fight him?'

'Oh yes, you have to fight him, and if you could endure that terrible battle, then you might know his secrets too.'

I thought about it, while the wind paced around outside.

'Is that all?'

'Pretty well all.'

'What happens if you lose the fight?'

'Into the drink with you, I should think, in pieces.'

'And if you beat him?'

'Well now,' said Ludo, drumming his fingers on the table, 'I don't know that, do I? Is there any – coffee?'

'You can have the bed,' I said, later. 'I'll sleep on the chair. It's fine. You're bigger. You'll be more comfortable.'

'That's kind of you Clip. But I'm not sleeping tonight.'

'I'd like to stay up with you, but I'm really...'

'I can see that. Leave the watch to me.'

'Right. Goodnight, then, Ludo. Don't – don't...' and then I did not know what to say.

'Don't worry. I might go for a little walk, later.'

'Take the torch. There're spare batteries in that drawer.'

'Thank you.'

'Don't fall off any cliffs.'

'Go to bed mun, you're swaying.'

I don't remember making it to the mattress. It was as if I had been drugged. The last I saw of him he was looking down at his hands, flexing his fingers.

I wake up in a darkness which is not quite dark and the door of my room is open and so is the door of the house. I go out, though I can't feel myself walking, and the air is warm and quite still. I take the high track up the middle of the island and the moon is low, light like old silver on the sea. Everywhere in the silence are figures. I can't see their faces but I know who some of them are. Friends and enemies, people I cared for and people I killed or whose deaths I caused, and people who died for me. They do not look at me as I pass – they are all staring away, the same way, towards the place I am going, to the end. As I come closer I hear noises. I hear cries.

At the very end of the island is the Wick, a cleft in the cliffs, a gorge where the sea, narrowly imprisoned, fights the rocks to be free. In the base of the cliffs, right in the tight throat of the Wick is a steep beach of stones, and though the shouts and the cries fill the whole chasm I know they are coming from there. Now I am crawling to the edge of the drop; I can feel the turf damp in my hands. There is something down there like a black mass alive, a struggle on the rattling stones. The moonlight cannot see it but I know there is a man down there with a horror like a huge beast and they are fighting to the death, fighting with great spears of driftwood, fighting with fists and rocks. There are knocking crashes at the sea's rim; I see sparks and hear detonations of stone.

Now I am holding my pistol. I am pointing down into the obscurity with my pistol and trying to take aim. If I can just get one sight of it, one shot at the thing, I will fire and I will not miss. But I fear to hit Ludo and the cries of pain are his and now I am desperately cursing because my clear shot never comes. At the sound of my cries there is a paleness down there and I see Ludo's face looking up. The huge darkness is looming over him.

'Get away, Clip!' he shouts, furious. 'Get out of it!'

The darkness is massive over him now, coiling itself for the deathblow. I shout to warn him and he turns but too slow and now I am pulling the trigger. The gun gives the dead-man's click and my heart stops.

A hand takes my shoulder and he turns me on my back. Behind him is a bright new blue. At first I think it is just the dazzle distorting him, but then I see he really is all bashed about. There is blood on his face and an egg instead of a cheekbone, purple and yellow and black. One eye is so battered it's practically shut. He is smiling.

'What happened to you?' he says.

'Ugh. What happened to you?'

'Get up mun, you can't be lying about on cliffs all day.'

He pulls me to my feet, printing stains of blood and earth on my palms. He is bigger, somehow, like the mad young giant of the docks. He is limping, I notice, and his left hand is pressed to his side.

'Look at it all!' he cries, and coughs blood, and still raises his good arm to the air, to the gulf skies and the forever of sea. 'What a day to be alive!'

He is missing at least three teeth, I reckon.

'Are we alive then?'

'Never more so! Come on!'

'Where to?'

'To the house! I need to wash – had a bit of a fall.'

He takes my arm and limps us away, never once looking back at the Wick.

'See anything interesting down there?'

'Oh yes. Yes, indeed!'

'What?'

'Oh! Things, Clip, things.'

'Tell me!'

'Oh, well. It was a dark and spooky night, after you went to sleep. And there were spirits abroad! Legions of them! All the hair was up all over me, even on my shins. And the thing I didn't tell you was – I had an appointment.'

'Who with?'

'Let's not name names.'

'I didn't hear anything.'

'You don't when people like that do their doings Clip! We're talking another realm here. Superyachts!'

'What?'

'Know what the latest craze is, among the big fish? Superyachts. Big as tankers, some of them. Your very own offshore island and it does thirty knots. Armed like frigates. Some of them are converted frigates, come to that. No taxes, no laws, every owner's a king. And they have choppers and mini-subs galore. Great...'

'Revolting, more like. Have you got one?'

'I might do, aye.'

'God, Ludo.' I paused and sat down on a stone. We were skirting the outcrop in the middle of the island, by the ruined farm. It was a day that might have fallen out of heaven. The larks were up.

'Anyway, I went to keep my appointment. He came in from the sea – helicopter, nice and low.'

'Tell me who he is.'

'Let's just call him the biggest fish, the banker-bandit king.'

'So what happens?'

'We meet on the beach. He puts his points, I put mine. We disagree.'

'Violently?'

'Violently, yes. So we try conclusions.'

'Meaning – you duff him up?'

'You could say I tried! Went for him alright. Here's the man even the super-class are super-scared of. The biggest piranha, right? You can be sure he knew his fists. It was a fair go like.'

'Who won?'

'You're getting ahead, Clip! He comes at me like a bloody polar bear. And I go for him. We grapple. He tries to squash the life out of me. His arms were timbers! His muscles were compressors! He could have mashed an armoured car. But didn't I grow up fighting? First my brothers, then everyone else? Don't I know a thing or two about the Unholy Trinity?'

'The Unholy Trinity?'

'Footwork, timing and hitting!'

'So you hit him?'

'Hit him? I was fixing to batter his head off and kick it out to sea!'

'And you won?'

'Not so fast Clip! I hit him and hit him and every time I landed one, one came hammering back. So I get some driftwood, and he gets a piece or two for himself, and we stood toe to toe and swung. There was going to be no begging. No quarter. No witnesses. Winner takes all and loser feeds the gulls.'

'Well you're still here, so I take it...'

'Nice of you. But I'm not so sure it's true.'

'You seem to have left some teeth behind.'

'Not just teeth. Not just teeth, oh no!'

'What, then?'

'Well I landed some beauties. So hard I could feel them going through me, and I heard my own ribs crack. I swung strikes and felt my own head battered sideways. I hit him with rocks and rocks hit me. I put him down and fell with him. I threw myself on him and pounded, felt my teeth break on stone. And then I up and dragged him and got us to a black rock pool, and forced his head right under. My mouth filled with salt water and there was a mallet of blows on my neck. And through the screaming and puke I shouted at him. You, you stinking mugger of women and children, you ruin, you arrogance, you poison. You deserve drowning and drowning's what you get.'

He paused and winced up at the mare's tails.

'Go on!'

'Well, I had a hand on the back of his head and one arm round his neck, and in the same way he held me. And as we fought and forced I swallowed water, and he did. I felt my strength going Clip. I heard rushing, my heart was pounding to the burst. I knew this was it. Fighting's very tiring, you know?'

'Yes.'

'Very tiring. And I thought, this is the man who emptied the treasury. This is the man by whose example the greedy have emptied the halls, impoverished the nation and brought the people to ruin. This is the man. And if I don't kill him now, then he kills me and all is lost and gone. This is the man who is happy to hoard more than he can ever need or spend, while children go hungry, and their fathers rot for lack of work, and their mothers can't sleep for agonies of worry, waiting for the next bailiff. This is the man who has blighted lives, killed futures, killed countries, while he sails away, laughing, drinking champagne, refining his pleasures. This is the man who makes whores of girls who should be students, of wives and mothers. This is the man who pays armies of people to safeguard his wealth – lawyers, accountants, bribe-takers, trash. This is the man who turns a nation's self-respect to numbers, and squanders it, and mocks the little people who are so poor and stupid they pay tax. This man has many names and many faces. He owns shops and media companies and phone companies; he calls tunes governments dance to, for his benefit alone. He uses his power to enslave the poor. He puts things in trusts, though he does not recognise the word – this is a jumped-up little horse trader who has held the world to ransom, scooped it and swagged it off-shore. This is a man who dares to look himself in the eye, because no one else quite can, except his own revolting kind. This is a man who wants killing, who wants drowning, his mouth full of sand and his lungs full of seawater. This is not a man, in fact, but a rabid beast of rapayne, and this foul thing I will kill.'

'So you killed him?'

'I was going to, Clip, but then he begged for mercy.'

'So you let him go?'

'He didn't just beg.'

'What then?'

'He said he would put it all back, and pay up, and tell his kind to do the same. He said he would be a model citizen. He swore fealty to me on the pain of the damnation of his eternal soul.'

'So you let him off?'

'I let him live. But I didn't let him off.'

'But he's gone? Back to his superyacht.'

'No, he hasn't gone.'

'Where is he then?'

'Can't you see him, clever Clip?'

'So now you know what you are doing, do you, Ludo?'

'I know exactly what must be done,' he said, with a grim and sudden calm. 'When I've had some tea I'm going to set right about it and it's going to be a tasty fight! And you're with me, aren't you? Well?'

Of course I was with him, I've always been with him, but I would not go. He knew I wouldn't, though he harangued me until the chopper came. He was still standing in the hatch and laughing, making 'Come with me!' gestures as Reda lifted off. That was the last time I saw him, peeling away across the sea. He stopped gesturing and waved madly then, and blew me kisses which I returned.

How he did whatever he set about I must leave for others to tell. I refused radios, though Stephen offered them, and computers and all. I decided to be perfectly content on the island: much happier with people I loved in thought than I could be in the awkwardness of seeing them, I concluded, and forgave myself, for there have always been hermits on this coast. All I knew of Ludo's progress was what I read in the night lights and the ships and the life of the bay. I saw the trade pick up when the tankers came and went. Tractors returned to wild fields on the headland; I saw more fishermen; in the summer the caravans came and I watched little boats batting the sea.

Knowing the ways in which he liked to fight I cannot imagine that Ludo's last battle was without its casualties. I imagine whosoever he set out to catch fought back, and kicked and griped on the hook. But I do know he loved his people, his ordinary people, and whatever he did was done for them. I am not sorry if this disappoints: if you seek to know more I commend your histories. If you dare it, you might look where Ludo did. You won't have to go all the way to the end of the land. This was only my story, and some of their's, the story of Ludo and Levello, and this is where it ends.

Katrin Williams, who was known as
Cut-lip Clip, the Prince's Pen.

Lludd and Llevelys
a synopsis

Lludd was the eldest of four: his brothers were Llevelys, Nynnyaw and Caswallawn. On the death of their father, Beli the Great, Lludd became king of Britain. He was just, generous and a great warrior. Of all his fortresses he loved London best; Lludd built up its walls and surrounded it with many towers. In time people called it Caer Lludd – which is how the city came by its name, Llundain, or London.

Of his brothers, Lludd was closest to the wise and handsome Llevelys. Llevelys heard that the king of France had died, leaving his daughter to inherit his realm. On Lludd's advice, Llevelys outfitted a fleet, sailed to France and sent messages to the royal court, proposing marriage to the princess. The match approved, Llevelys married the princess and assumed the crown. He ruled with honesty and dignity.

In time three plagues fell over the islands of Britain. The first was the coming of the Corannyeid, a people so sophisticated that there was no conversation anywhere in the country that they could not hear, provided the wind could catch it: none could rise against them. The second plague was a scream, heard everywhere every May-eve, which drove people and animals mad. The third was the disappearance of all the provisions from the king's courts: however much was stored, nothing would remain in the morning.

Perplexed and alarmed, Lludd sailed in secret to ask Llevelys for advice. Llevelys, ignorant of Lludd's intentions, met him with many ships. Leaving his fleet behind, Lludd met his brother alone and embraced him. Llevelys used a bronze horn to speak to Lludd so that the wind would not catch their words, but everything that was said into the horn came out hateful and contrary. Llevelys realised the horn was cursed. He washed it through with wine, which drove out its devil and allowed the brothers to speak.

Llevelys gave Lludd some insects and instructed him to mix them with water. If Lludd summoned all the peoples of Britain, he said, and threw the mixture over them, only the Corannyeid would be poisoned. The second plague, Llevelys explained, was caused by two dragons – one British and one foreign, which screamed as they fought. He told Lludd to dig a pit in the exact centre of Britain, in Oxford, and to bury a vat of mead in it, covered by a silk sheet. The dragons would fight in terrible forms until they were exhausted, whereupon they would fall into the sheet in the shapes of two little pigs. They would sink into the mead, drink it and fall asleep. Lludd should wrap them in the sheet, lock them in a stone chest and bury them in the safest place in Britain. The third plague was caused by a giant, a magician, Llevelys said, who cast spells to send everyone to sleep. He advised Lludd to use a vat of cold water to stay awake, and keep watch.

Lludd returned to his land, summoned his people, and doused them with the mixture Llevelys had provided. All the Corannyeid perished but the British were unharmed. Then Lludd dug a pit in Oxford and prepared it as Llevelys had advised. The dragons came and fought until they dropped into the sheet, and down into the mead, where they slept. Lludd wrapped them up and buried them in Dinas Emreis. Finally, Lludd ordered a feast to be laid out and a vat of cold water set near. Everyone fell asleep but Lludd, who immersed himself repeatedly. At last a huge man in armour appeared and began to stow the feast in his basket. Lludd was amazed by how much the basket could hold. He challenged the giant and fought him, until the sparks flew from their weapons. It was a terrible struggle but destiny gave victory to Lludd. The giant begged for mercy, promising to restore all he had taken and swearing to be Lludd's faithful follower thereafter. Lludd accepted.

In this way Lludd rid Britain of the three plagues. Afterwards he ruled in peace and prosperity for as long as he lived. This tale is called the Adventure of Lludd and Llevelys, and here it ends.

Synopsis:
for the full story see *The Mabinogion, A New Translation*
by Sioned Davies (Oxford World's Classics, 2007).

Afterword

On the wall of one of the classrooms of my childhood was a timeline of Welsh literature, beginning in the corner of the room with the *Mabinogion*. It seemed an appropriately dense and twisting root: the small print described branches and boars, Romans, cauldrons, Arthur, Irish links, Celts. Among the books set by my teachers the *Mabinogion* never featured. I bought a dull-jacketed edition, without introduction or notes – which I soon missed. It was like reading a spell book, half in runes, without a key. One imagined listeners in some age of dark, nodding at symbolisms and references only rare scholars might now understand. It was this series of Seren's which took me back to the stories. And then came the email from Penny Thomas, editor of this series. Bless my luck, 'Lludd and Llevelys' had not been taken by another writer. It was instantly the one I wanted.

Their story barely runs to five pages and its very brevity makes the brothers more monumental. Lludd, with all his heroic qualities, adds a dimension not much seen in heroes, except when its absence is a tragic flaw – he listens. And he has a wise counsellor in his brother. One of the great pleasures of my life is my relationship with a wise brother. The human crack in the smooth old shell of the tale, their argument – when the brothers try to speak through a horn, and all comes out contrary until Llevelys washes it clean with wine – was the first aperture through which I saw characters I recognised, and therefore a story. Although the judgement of leaders as great or not great is history's prerogative, I have consciously seen only one sure star, in Nelson Mandela – though a case could be made for Mikhail Gorbachev. Lludd – Ludo, as he became – could not be a Mandela, but I tried to give him some of the playfulness, the humour and the sense of historic purpose that one of Mandela's fellow prisoners once described to me, recalling his time on Robben Island with the liberator of South Africa. I addressed that challenge, the description of a great man, with the sense of needing someone like that fellow prisoner, who could recall him first-hand.

The myth presents its plot as a gift to any re-teller. You cannot help but feel that the five pages we have left are a worn-down nub of a gripping epic. Invasion, civil strife and crisis – and all beaten by a leader's technology, cunning and strength: how those old bards must have had them craning forward in the firelight while they told it! The key line, the fulcrum about which the whole thing turns, sounds as though it has struck all its listeners with equal force and so survived every telling: the description of the power of the Corannyeid. 'There was no conversation anywhere in the island, however hushed, that they did not hear, provided the wind caught it; consequently no harm could be done to them.' To today's reader that can only mean surveillance, certainly to a citizen of the same island, which has become the most snooped-on in the world. I did not have to look far for examples of people who have become the prey of our most terrible technologies.

The two dragons seemed to me to be two faiths but they might just as easily have been two tribes – one is described as 'foreign'; the other is 'your dragon', as Llevelys tells Lludd. The way they are disposed of together, buried in an eternal embrace, seemed rather touching and appropriate: how has this island ever prospered except by an embrace (sometimes exploitative, but sometimes also noble) of the world? The solution to the dragons' conflict is a mingling, an inter-marriage: time, above all. Their reduction, in the tale, from vast monsters to two little pigs is a wonderfully incisive – and somehow very Welsh – take-down: what are the great trumpeting screams of competing faiths, at root, but the amplified grunting of the little pigs of ego inside mortal demagogues? Similarly, the giant who empties the kingdom's cellars is these days a familiar force: nebulous, working invisibly, casting sleep and ignorance over its victims.

Although *The Prince's Pen* is necessarily an extrapolation, it intentionally departs from the spirit and the letter of the original only once, in the brothers' solution to the Corannyeid. This story puns on 'bug', rather than depicting the full horror of the myth, in which biological (and presumably gene-based) warfare is used, in a monstrously casual and effective way. Perhaps consequently it misses an opportunity to explore a potential nightmare of the near-future. I don't regret it: some things are too hideous to contemplate. The solution works in the myth only because the Corannyeid descend – as original audiences would have understood – from the fairy folk of Breton legend. Fortunately, we no longer have the luxury of quite being able to believe in the dehumanisation of our foes.

Acknowledgements

The 'Mitchell' referred to is David Mitchell; the book is his *The Thousand Autumns of Jacob de Zoet.* All my love and thanks to John and Sally Clare. Many thanks to the editorial and production staff at Seren, particularly Penny Thomas. Thank you, Zoe Waldie and Mohsen Shah, and thank you, Manu at the Oberdan Cafe. And thank you, Merlin Hughes, Roger Couhig, Alexander Clare and Rebecca Shooter. This is for you, with love.

GWYNETH LEWIS
THE MEAT TREE

A dangerous tale of desire, DNA, incest and flowers plays out within the wreckage of an ancient spaceship in *The Meat Tree*, an absorbing retelling of one of the best-known Welsh myths by prizewinning writer and poet, Gwyneth Lewis.

An elderly investigator and his female apprentice hope to extract the fate of the ship's crew from its antiquated virtual reality game system, but their empirical approach falters as the story tangles with their own imagination.

By imposing a distance of another 200 years and millions of light years between the reader and the medieval myth, Gwyneth Lewis brings the magical tale of Blodeuwedd, a woman made of flowers, closer than ever before: maybe uncomfortably so.

After all, what man has any idea how sap burns in the veins of a woman?

Gwyneth Lewis was the first National Poet of Wales, 2005-6. She has published seven books of poetry in Welsh and English, the most recent of which is *A Hospital Odyssey*. *Parables and Faxes* won the Aldeburgh Poetry Prize and was also shortlisted for the Forward, as was *Zero Gravity*. Her non-fiction books are *Sunbathing in the Rain: A Cheerful Book on Depression* (shortlisted for the Mind Book of the Year) and *Two in a Boat: A Marital Voyage*.

OWEN SHEERS
WHITE RAVENS

"Hauntingly imaginative..." – Dannie Abse

Two stories, two different times, but the thread of an ancient tale runs through the lives of twenty-first-century farmer's daughter Rhian and the mysterious Branwen... Wounded in Italy, Matthew O'Connell is seeing out WWII in a secret government department spreading rumours and myths to the enemy. But when he's given the bizarre task of escorting a box containing six raven chicks from a remote hill farm in Wales to the Tower of London, he becomes part of a story over which he seems to have no control.

Based on the Mabinogion story 'Branwen, Daughter of Llyr', *White Ravens* is a haunting novella from an award-winning writer.

Owen Sheers is the author of two poetry collections, *The Blue Book* and *Skirrid Hill* (both Seren); a Zimbabwean travel narrative, *The Dust Diaries* (Welsh Book of the Year 2005); and a novel, *Resistance*, shortlisted for the Writers' Guild Best Book Award. *A Poet's Guide to Britain* is the accompanying anthology to Owen's BBC 4 series.

RUSSELL CELYN JONES
THE NINTH WAVE

"A brilliantly-imagined vision of the near future...
one of his finest achievements." – Jonathan Coe

Pwyll, a young Welsh ruler in a post-oil world, finds his inherited status hard to take. And he's never quite sure how he's drawn into murdering his future wife's fiancé, losing his only son and switching beds with the king of the underworld. In this bizarrely upside-down, medieval world of the near future, life is cheap and the surf is amazing; but you need a horse to get home again down the M4.

Based on the Mabinogion story 'Pwyll, Lord of Dyfed', *The Ninth Wave* is an eerie and compelling mix of past, present and future. Russell Celyn Jones swops the magical for the psychological, the courtly for the post-feminist and goes back to Swansea Bay to complete some unfinished business.

Russell Celyn Jones is the author of six novels. He has won the David Higham Prize, the Society of Authors Award, and the Weishanhu Award (China). He is a regular reviewer for several national newspapers and is Professor of Creative Writing at Birkbeck College, London.

NIALL GRIFFITHS
THE DREAMS OF MAX & RONNIE

There's war and carnage abroad and Iraq-bound squaddie Ronnie is out with his mates 'forgetting what has yet to happen'. He takes something dodgy and falls asleep for three nights in a filthy hovel where he has the strangest of dreams, watching the tattooed tribes of modern Britain surrounding a grinning man playing war games.

Meanwhile gangsta Max is fed up with life in his favourite Cardiff nightclub, Rome, and chases a vision of the perfect woman in far-flung parts of his country. But as Max loses his heart, his followers fear he may be losing his touch.

Niall Griffiths' retellings of two dream myths from the medieval Welsh Mabinogion cycle reveal an astonishingly contemporary and satirical resonance. Arthurian legend merges with its twenty-first century counterpart in a biting commentary on leadership, conflict and the divisions in British society.

Niall Griffiths was born in Liverpool in 1966, studied English, and now lives and works in Aberystwyth. His novels include *Grits*, *Sheepshagger, Kelly and Victor* and *Stump*, which won Wales Book of the Year, and *Runt*. His non-fiction includes *Real Aberystwyth* and *Real Liverpool*. He also writes reviews, radio plays and travel pieces.

FFLUR DAFYDD
THE WHITE TRAIL

Life is tough for Cilydd after his heavily pregnant wife vanishes in a supermarket one wintry afternoon. And his private-eye cousin Arthur doesn't appear to be helping much.

The trail leads them to a pigsty, a cliff edge and a bloody warning that Cilydd must never marry again. But eventually the unlikely hero finds himself on a new and dangerous quest – a hunt for the son he never knew, a meeting with a beautiful and mysterious girl, and a glimpse inside the House of the Missing.

In this contemporary retelling from Seren's New Stories from the Mabinogion series, award-winning writer Fflur Dafydd transforms the medieval Welsh Arthurian myth of Culhwch and Olwen into a twenty-first-century quest for love and revenge.

Fflur Dafydd is the author of four novels and one short story collection. She won the Oxfam Hay Emerging Writer of the Year Award 2009 and is the first female author ever to have won both the Prose Medal and the Daniel Owen Memorial Prize at the National Eisteddfod. She has also released three albums as a singer-songwriter and was named BBC Radio Cymru Female Artist of the Year in 2010. She lectures in Creative Writing at Swansea University and lives in Carmarthen with her husband and daughter.